ALICE'S MIND

A Story of Mind and Thought Manipulation

Derek Finn

frogsnotpigeons

ISBN-13: 9798696768274
ISBN-10: 1477123456

Cover design by: frogsnotpigeons
Library of Congress Control Number: 2018675309
Printed in the United States of America

CONTENTS

ALICE'S MIND

INTRODUCTION

Alice Braithward had already lived a long time. Sometimes, she felt like she was a dinosaur, or a living fossil of a time long gone. Sometimes, she felt just like a grandmother. She was a successful businesswoman in her own right and had out survived many of her friends, peers and competitors. She did not put this down to chance or luck, but rather to will power and hard work. She attributed her success to no one else except herself.

Alice was fascinated with the behaviour of others and loved people watching. She could think of nothing better than when someone challenged or engaged with her and revelled in strategic power plays. And every interaction was a game to Alice. Either she was going to win, or she was going to lose. And Alice B did not like to lose.

Although she loved the cut and thrust of the business world, she also had a dark side to her. She was overconfident to the point of arrogance and she showed little or no empathy for others. She was ruthless and had no tolerance for excuses or under performance.

Related to her people watching fascination, she believed that her lucid dreams were a way for her to enter and experience others life's. She recorded her dreams and wrote them up in her journal for future reflection. Often mixing fantasy and reality. She saw herself as a watcher of others, of those not as fortunate as herself. Of those who did not have her mind capacity.

Although in her eightieth year, she hated that she was old. She saw this as her weakness that could be exploited by others more youthful, more agile than her. She could not abide the senile old woman viewpoint and usually punished harshly anyone who assumed this about her.

In her mind, she wanted to live forever and saw her aging as a problem that needed to be solved. Alice was pre-occupied with brain function and specifically why neurocognitive decline was considered inevitable as part of the aging process. EEG scans of her brain wave patterns showed a stable mean alpha frequency of 12Hz. This was unusual for a woman in her eighties who demonstrated that even with reduced brain volume and separation of the brain hemispheres, she still had normal adult brain activity. She showed completely normal function of pre-frontal cortex that controlled attention and decision making. In parallel, her memory was also excellent.

Alice believed that aging was not an inevitable course of decline. It was not a disease but a biological process that could be influenced. There is no gene or genetic marker that triggers a biological countdown clock and although the human life span was increasing through advances in disease treatment, improved diet and living conditions, cognitive decline had quickly becoming the limiting factor. After all, there was no benefit to living longer if there was no quality of life. Cognitive diseases such as Alzheimer's and associated memory loss, robbed people of life quality.

Alice, and her research company Time Shift Inc considered the functional decline in neurotransmitter metabolism to be the root cause of lower brain activity detected as part of the healthy aging process. This reduction in cognitive function correlated with a slowing of brain wave frequency, and that low alpha power, correlates with neurocognitive decline.

Recent technology advances in neuroscience enabled the mapping of brain regions that showed the electrical communication pathways of the brain itself. This fascinated Alice to the point of becoming a fixation for her.

She believed that managing and manipulation of neuronal pathway communication in the brain could lead to extending cognitive function in healthy aging. She also believed that every individual transmitted and received low frequency signals that were hitherto undetectable. Frequency, she believed, was how humans communicate emotions and feelings without speaking.

The following chapters indulge Alice Braithward and her visits to other lives. Her watching of others as they deal with traumatic experiences or events in the moment or through recalled experience. Sometimes, those watched, sense that someone is watching as though a feeling or a Deja vu experience.

Or perhaps, they just detect the low frequency signal of someone else present.

Ultimately, Alice solves her problem by making it someone else's.

THE SHOP

22 Weeks Ago.

The people disappearing business is around for a long time. Certainly not unique, but perhaps not as mainstream visible as other businesses. As a confidential service, it is not to be found on the town high street.

The Disappearing Shop was set up ten years ago by founder and current Chairperson, Alice Braithward, and recently became part of larger interest group that has served many clients over the years. TDS does not get customer reviews, nor do they get return customer business. They are not rated on Trust Pilot and do not have a Facebook or Instagram page.

The TDS client base is extremely broad. We get all sorts of people both young and old. But all of them have one thing in common. They want to disappear. The first challenge of course, is to find your local Disappearing Shop. As much as we would like to, we do not advertise on mainstream social media platforms and our customers usually find us through asking the right people or associate referrals.

TDS does not operate from a fixed location and instead finds it advantageous to have a mobile office base. And, once you have found our shop, the process becomes strictly confidential after that on a need to know basis.

We start with a client interview. It is critical that we have a collective understanding of the objective and the client understands our delivery terms and conditions. All too often, people go to the effort and expense of finding us only to discover that they cannot afford our offering. And I do not mean in financial terms, but instead the terms and conditions of our service that can put some clients off. For example, we do not offer cooling off periods or insurance indemnity, neither do we offer refunds.

Once you are gone under our service, you do not come back under any circumstance. I am still surprised to this day how many clients turn up and want to disappear for a 'while' or a year or some other defined term. We are not in the holiday business and do not cater for temporary disappearances. Once your gone – your gone. You never come back.

Susan Birchfield was referred to our shop by a trusted inter-mediate and we arranged our first client meeting. By first impres-sions, Susan appeared as a professional young woman probably in her early to mid-thirties. She was well dressed. Business casual attire and wore a pair of dark sunglasses. I always cringe when potential new customers arrive in sunglasses. Our professional opinion is that they do not really work as a disguise and have limited function outside of the design purpose of keeping the sun out of your eyes.

Susan was escorted to my office and we did the usual meet and greets. Polite, soft handshake and I invited her to take a seat. I did notice her manicured hands and what appeared an expensive watch that gave the impression of disposable income. Of course, we never judge a client on looks. Often, what you see is not what you get.

'Thank you, Susan, for considering our service.' I opened. 'Can you tell me something about yourself and perhaps what brings you here today?'

Susan gave me an overview of her business and financial diffi-culties explaining that she had entered some questionable busi-ness contracts with some very shady characters that she could no longer extricate herself from. I hear this a lot in this line of work. Unusual in a young woman perhaps, but nonetheless, a common disappearance driver.

'Please do continue Susan.' I invited.

'I've come to the end of who I am. I don't have an option but to disappear for good and start somewhere else, new name, new identity.' She said.

'You do realise Susan, that there is no going back. The process cannot be reversed?'

'Yes. I understand' she affirmed.

I explained to Susan that this was an initial exploratory meeting and that I will contact her in due course. That is, if or when, there will be a second meeting. If I do not make contact in the coming weeks, it means that we will not do business together. This always catches the client by surprise. But we would not be doing our job if we did not run background verification on all our clients.

Firstly, the background checks are always incredibly detailed. It is amazing sometimes how much information people put on social media platforms about themselves that is readily accessible by anyone. A quick search for Susan and we have multiple website hits with photos, family, and a few friends. This is not really a problem for us. We have software apps that search out and blitz online profiles. Once cleaned up, it can be made appear that the person never existed.

Secondly, we need to verify the client's story about business and financial difficulties. This is always more complicated as we need to protect our client while at the same time give ourselves the assurance that all is as explained. Despite GDPR, financial institute records, credit reports and employment records are easily obtained and provide a good insight to the client and their motivations for using our service. During this financial discovery phase, the clients banking records are provided for verification by our agents. It also means that we can check that the client has the means to pay for our service. After all, we are not a charity business and can be, for some, expensive.

However, in this client case, Susan has sufficient funds on hand in various checking accounts that were guaranteed by a third-party benefactor. We also note significant debt accounts and imminent foreclosure notices from more than one financial institution.

Thirdly. Travel and medical history are always a bit trickier. Local authority and health care insiders are an expensive but necessary resource. However, we have never found any problems recruiting low paid administration staff in these services.

Knowing what information is required and where it can be obtained can be acquired for relatively small outlay. Of course, we prefer clients who do not have extensive medical history or ongoing medical conditions.

Prescription continuations for someone who has disappeared is a potential trace connection to the past. But our experience is that patients who do not turn up for future medical appointments are not looked for beyond a phone call to a previously held number on file.

Back at the office, the Chairperson and the associates consult on the findings of the various surveys and risk factors identified. Susan appears on the face of investigations to date, a 'low risk' disappearance. Her age profile is a slight concern. Youngish clients typically have more contacts in terms of friends and family than older clients. In simple terms, more people look for missing young people. Perhaps a societal condition, but our experience is that people do not look extremely hard or long for older people who disappear.

In this case, Susan's deep financial difficulties and family divisions offset some of the age profile risk. People who have financial difficulties tend to disappear more often. This creates a certain bias on the part of investigative agencies who see these individual disappearances as assumed flight and hide cases. This is the perfect cover for a business of our nature. That is to 'disappear' our client successfully.

It is collectively decided by the decision board that we will proceed with Susan as a suitable client for our business. We go through multiple possible approaches and finally decide on the best approach for this client with the lowest risk and ease of implementation. A dedicated Project Manager, Philip Burns, is assigned who will be responsible for planning, schedule development and application phases. Philip is new to the role of Project Manager but highly regarded by the business and a personal selection of our Chairwoman.

Susan was informed and seemed genuinely delighted with the acceptance. Her excitement was slightly contagious, and the office set about making the detailed arrangements to make Susan's successful disappearance happen.

Over the coming weeks the team met with Susan. She had loads of new ideas about her new identity and what new life she would like to have post disappearance. Her enthusiasm was overwhelming at times and it was difficult to contain her. It was explained multiple times to her that there was no coming back and that this was a once in a lifetime transaction that could not be reversed. She gleefully accepted and signed all necessary release forms placed before her.

On the 28th, two days before the planned day of disappearance, Susan made her final payment for our service. We are a cash only business and of course always insist on payment in advance. Delivery of various automated apps to wipe client records were launched on a delayed timer to activate on midnight of the prescribed target date. This is partially precautionary but ensures that any email communication history is wiped from the email servers. Susan is then presented with the final letter to sign. This letter carefully outlines to any remaining family and interested local authorities why she has decided to opt to disappear. It is always a very emotional letter that we have prepared for clients many times.

Other documents exchanged are passport and driving licence. Essentially, any photo identification that has her original name on it. We retain the client originals and dispose of them promptly after the event.

On the final day, Susan is collected at a pre-agreed pick up location. As usual, her car is parked up in a laneway selected for privacy and overhung by trees to prevent CCTV or overhead visual intrusions. Her car is left unlocked, Susan gets into a nontraceable vehicle and is driven by one of our associates to the 'extraction' point. This is always a lonely isolated location as witnesses can be problematic later.

And that is it essentially. Normally, final emails and letters of goodbye signed by the client trigger a search. It takes a couple of days before Susan is washed up down river and the case is closed.

Disappeared for ever with no come back.

DEATH BY DESIGN

'I'd love to go on a cruise this year' Kimberly said gleefully looking across the breakfast table to her husband. Doctor David Ryan is a neurologist working at Saint James's Hospital and highly regarded in his field. He ignores his wife's comment. He has heard it many times. In his mind, he thinks of his wife as a woman of shallow values who spends most of her days pruning, watching reality television and then talking about others to anyone who will listen.

Kimberly's source of income is her husband who spends his time working between both private and public consultancy practices that she can live the lifestyle she is entitled to. And so, it is for the last twenty years or more. Of course, enough is never enough and Kimberly must constantly push her husband to do more, earn more, work harder to sustain her lifestyle and the standard she has become accustomed to.

'Cruising the Caribbean – that's where we are going on holidays this year!' exclaims the Wife. The husband folds his paper and gets up from the kitchen table. 'I have to get off to work' he mutters before putting on his overcoat and placing the newspaper under his arm heading out the front door.

Dr Ryan is a sensible man. He does not really have any excesses beyond his work commitment. He has extended himself on his mortgage after buying an oversized and equally overvalued property a couple of years ago that is now part of a declining market. But it kept Kimberly happy for a short while anyway. The financial pressure of the mortgage and the cost of living up to Kimberley's expectations worried Dr Ryan for some time now. The debt is mounting steadily and there is an inevitable point of no return when income is less than outgoings. He often thinks that he is worth more dead than alive with all the joint life insurances and multiple policies. A societal necessity to lenders of high value debt.

A busy work load that day, the Doctor is heavily pre-occupied with the health problems of others. His final appointment that day was the ever young eighty-year-old Mrs Alice Braithward. Despite her years, Alice, was a neuroscience miracle and an interesting conversationalist. Her routine visits to check her mental acuity always followed by a cup of tea and a discussion on world affairs. Tonight, Dr Ryan shared the plans for a cruise holiday and his own growing feelings of contempt for his wife's narrow view of the world. Dr Ryan felt some relief from being able to discuss his worries openly with someone who was non-judgemental of the situation that he found himself in.

Working through till late, the doctor eventually puts back on his coat to make the return journey back to his fancy house on the hill. Arriving in through the large gates and up the gravel driveway he parks outside his front door. As he turns off the ignition, he sits momentarily looking at the palatial house that has become such a burden on his life. The hesitation to enter clears his fogged mind and he walks up the steps to the front door.

On entering, the house is awash with the lights on in every room. A fleeting thought of the size of this house's carbon footprint crossed his mind.

'Your late' is the call that greets him from the dining room. Kimberly walks towards him and places a deftly welcome kiss to his cheek. 'I have some great news to tell you' she exclaims with excitement in her eyes. 'I went into my friends travel agents and got a great bargain on a holiday deal'.

'Oh?' feigns the Doctor inquisitively. Placing his coat over the back of a nearby chair and his briefcase to the floor.

'Yes – we are going on the cruise that you have always wanted!'

'Really. The cruise that I always wanted?' he asks. Slightly more curious.

'Yes – David. Please do pay attention when you come home. I'm not one of your patients you know'.

'What have you done Kimberly? You know that I have to work to pay for this house and we can't afford expensive holidays this year'.

'Don't be so selfish David. I got a great last-minute discount and its already booked so I do not want to hear you complaining about it. We are going next month so get your understudy to cover for you.'

No more to be said. He looks down at the non-refundable credit card receipt for a mini cruise around the Gulf of Mexico. Not sure whether to laugh or cry he quietly picks up his fork and starts on his reheated dinner plate.

Over the next few weeks, the Doctor's mood improves as Kimberly is busy organizing and credit purchasing the compulsory holiday attire necessary for the wife of a Doctor about to head off on a cruise holiday to the Caribbean. Of course, one must look a certain way for a cruise ship and you never know who else might be on the cruise. This will be the holiday of the year in so many ways for both of them.

Doctor Ryan throws himself into his work clearing as many of the more seriously afflicted patients as he can. He thinks it is not fair to have too much work for his understudy during his vacation absence. At the same time, a part of him is looking forward to this cruise. In the evenings, he researches the stop points of the cruise and interesting facts on the ship. Strikingly, obscure facts. The Gulf of Mexico has numerous types of sharks in its waters. Did you know that every year people go missing from cruise ships never to be found? Strangely, the Doctor is starting to warm to this cruise holiday after all.

On arrival, at the boarding port, the couple are escorted aboard. David only too happy that the porters have taken over the loading of the luggage. Many heavy suitcases contain many new dresses and outfits with fashion labels. David wonders will she even get to wear all of them. Afterall, he is still wearing what he had last year. No new expensive outfits for him.

A few days later and the cruise is well underway. This is a big ship and David has taken to noting the positions and locations of the many security camera's dotted around the ship deck. All the while his wife is sunbathing on the lounge deck, so he has the time to walk the decks at his own leisure. Strangely comforting and relaxing in its own way.

Kimberly is pre-occupied with the attention from one of the crew members who is more than happy to keep serving her the latest and greatest of cocktails. David had decided that his financial rescue plan will start tonight.

The Captain's dinner that night is a lavish affair. An opportunity for the guests to break out the designer labels and show off their wealth. Real or not does not seem to matter to most. David steadies his resolve with a couple of drinks himself. Post main course and pre-desert, David leans into Kimberly to suggest a stroll top side along the deck. This will be a quiet time; he thinks as most of the passengers and crew are preoccupied. And he knows exactly the part of the deck he will show Kimberly.

Walking hand in hand the couple take in the moonlit night. The noise of the ship as it makes its way through the water is almost hypnotic. Stopping at a preselected location, not covered by the CCTV coverage. David invites his lovely Kimberly to look over the edge of the railing.

Holding the rail, she peers down on the dark ocean broken only by the white of the surge breaking itself needlessly against the steel hull of the vessel. David thinks to himself how well she looks in this light in her fabulous ball dress that probably cost more than he earns in a month.

Standing close to her, he readies himself to put his plan into action. He draws a breath when suddenly he sees the outline of one of the cabin crew approach him quickly. Kimberly takes a step back and David is suddenly hoisted beyond the top rail. As he falls, he looks back to see his wife's face as she watches silently his descent towards the dark ocean. His final thoughts of his patient Alice Braithward and her warnings about opportunity blind to threats.

The surge of the boat is strong. Anything in the water is dragged immediately under the boat and washed through at the back of the boat like a giant washing machine. Churned shark food, Dr Ryan is never to be found again.

Financial problem solved thinks Kimberly as she hears the deafening sound of man over-board ring out across the deck.

MATURITY

20 Weeks ago

Eva always suspected that Jim had a second women on the go. While on his many business trips he was often uncontactable for days on end. He just would not answer his calls. He did not check his messages and made the excuse that his message inbox was full. I mean, who has a full message inbox nowadays? She had a feeling in her stomach that he was with someone else.

Eva even got others to ask him also, but he always denied it. One time, when he was on the missing list again, she texted his mother. But she had also not heard from Jim and said that she could not contact him either. Jim was angry with Eva for asking about him with his mother. He told her to stop panicking and not to worry his aging mother again. He also did not like it that Eva called him Jim making out that it was disrespectful for her to call him the same name as everyone else.

Philip Burns came across to Eva as the gentleman type in the pub. A bit older than her. She placed him in his early thirties or forties. A professional with a career job she thought.

With her best girlfriend, she sat at a small table where the waiter placed two glasses of house white before the two girls. Not really her drink, she found it bitter, and strong, but it got easier after the first glass. Eva had only started drinking wine after her mother had died suddenly a few months back. It was her mother's favourite drink and she had become a bit of a wine buff before she had passed.

Eva found it nice though that an older man was interested in her. After all these years, she thought, I am still attractive when I want to be. She lifted her second glass of wine and cheered it towards Philip sitting on a bar stool close by their table. He smiled back and picked up his drink to come over to the girl's table.

'Will you marry me?' he asked while sliding his hand across her back deftly.

Eva nearly choked on her Chardonnay. 'Very original chat up line' she said.

He took her left hand. 'What about a date then?'

Her face turned bright red. He smiled broadly as he pulled a chair up beside her at the table. He placed his hand on her leg. Just a little too high.

Eva found Philip a handsome man. Something James Bond about him but not quite the full Monty. He was not really her type. But still. He was smart and just at that moment in her life, knew exactly what to say. He gave her a feeling that she was the most beautiful woman in the world. Philip was confident and knew about everything. He knew what he wanted. From the first moment they met there was absolutely no doubt. He wanted Eva. And he was going to get her.

Eva's friend looked across and told her with her eyes her disapproval of her flirting. Philip also sensed the friend's disapproval and diplomatically asked if they would like a refill. Eva's friend declined abruptly that signalled the end of conversation.

When Jim arrived home the following day from his 'business trip' Eva was glad to see him home but slightly less so than previous. He dropped his bag of washing into the wash basket ready for the wash fairy to clean and iron for him before his next business trip.

'Everything all right with you?' he asked reading her body language.

'Yes of course. Why wouldn't it be?' she responded curtly.

Jim knew her well and did not respond to the question knowing that it would open a row that he did not want. He sat down in front of the television and finding the remote changed the channel to CNN News. Seems that anything to do with a Donald Trump Interview could grab his attention faster.

Eva's annoyance seethed into a rising anger that had no reason but was fully justified in her own mind.

'So, where have you been all day?' she asked.

'Oh, nowhere. Late meetings and some important decisions took longer than expected' he said still holding the remote control in his hand waving it in a circle pattern as though to lasso some invisible animal.

'Really? I don't know any place called nowhere.'

'Don't be a silly girl. I'm just in the door from work and already your quizzing me'.

Eva felt a knot in her stomach as she raged slowly at his dismissive tone. I do not deserve to be treated like this she thought to herself. She picked up post that had come in earlier and dropped it on the table in front of him.

'This arrived for you this morning.' she said curtly.

'Ok. I'll look at it later.'

'Why can't you look at it now?'

Jim quickly placed the remote on the coffee table and snapped up the letter. He tore it open and removed the typed letter inside. 'It's a statement from the bank. Are you satisfied now? What else would you like me to do – should I go and paint the Kitchen?' he roared as he turned back to his news updates about China or something else.

'What is wrong with you?' Eva roared back at him standing between him and television.

He did not respond and instead tried to stare around her legs to see the screen. This broke her will power and she stormed off out of the room slamming the door off the hinges so loud so that the neighbours could hear two houses away.

Eva flipped open her phone cover and was about to message her best girlfriend when she noticed five messages from Philip, her admirer. She sat on the edge of the bed and scanned the messages in quick succession. Eva quickly threw on her favourite jacket and ran down the stairs to the hallway.

'Where are you going? You need to be back here by....' shouted Jim from his leather cushioned throne.

'Out' was the only response he was getting as she slammed the front door on the way. How dare he try and tell me what time I need to be anywhere. She thought angrily to herself.

Reaching the corner near McDonalds, Eva could see Philip was waiting for her. His trench coat made him look like an extra from an old detective movie that she had not seen for a long time.

'Great to see you – and you do look great' he said as Eva approached him. Exactly what she needed to hear. He bent forward and kissed her on the cheek. She blushed up.

'Where would you like to go?' he asked.

'Maybe we can have something quick to eat here?' Eva said without thinking looking back at the almost empty McDonalds.

Philip placed a hand across her shoulders and turned her the opposite direction. 'Let's go this way for a quiet drink. I know just the place.'

Eva skipped along beside him feeling exhilarated and excited at the same time. The couple turned a few corners and she realised quickly that she did not know where they were. Philip stopped at a small dingy looking terrace house door and fumbled around for a key.

'What is this place?' she asked. 'I thought we were going for a drink?'

Philip was busy though searching through his raincoat pocket for a key. He seemed anxious to get inside quickly. He caught hold of Eva's arm with his free hand as though to make sure she was still there.

'Philip is this where you live?' she asked again becoming slightly nervous now.

At this point he had the key in the small yale lock and was trying desperately to turn the key. Left, then right, then left while pushing and pulling it at the same time. At the same time, he was looking up and down the dark street to see if anyone was watching. By now, Eva was starting to get nervous.

'Philip, you are frightening me?' she shouted. This time his response shocked her.

'Shut up you stupid little girl'.

Eva pulled back quickly trying to free herself from Philip's hold. He held on tighter. She pulled again to eventually break free and started to run back towards the lights.

He followed. She could hear his heavy shoe steps behind that ultimately slowed him down. Coming to the corner, she turned and could see the lights of McDonalds in the distance and knew that there would be others around that she would be safe.

Eva flipped open her phone. Frequent contact name 'Jim' and dialled the number. Jim answered promptly. 'Where are you?' came back the concerned voice.

'I'm so sorry Dad' tears streaming down her face. 'I'm outside McDonalds on the High Street.'

'I'll be there straight away' he said.

COUNSELLING PHILIP

Attending the first counselling session of the week is always difficult. Philip Burns reaffirmed in his mind that it is just the summoning of the courage to get out there and do it. To speak to a stranger without judging or being judged. This takes a lot of effort and attention focus to empathically listen and respond to another person.

Most people do not like to be judged and do not take criticism too well either. But Philip remembered being told some time ago that if you at least recognise your limitations, then your halfway there to accepting them. Or something along those lines. Philip always did find it difficult to understand these expressions. Meaningless metaphors abound in this profession.

The front of the clinic reminds you why you are here. Philip wondered if the architects gave up on design at the front door of these treatment centres. The white aluminium framed double door communicates 'I don't give a fuck. Welcome to psychotherapy. Looser.'

Philip had a problem all his life. Or at least as long as he could remember. His childhood was shaped in a context of domestic violence predicated in alcoholism.

Now in his early twenties he was considered sociopathic and could be extremely aggressive. Recently though, he had managed to get a job and under medication seemed to be making some progress in controlling his anger outburst.

Philip entered the clinic that morning for his weekly counselling session as arranged and a condition of his empathic employer. He was not particularly bothered either way. He found the sessions to be a time nuisance, or perhaps an inconvenience that got him across town in a morning. Of course, there were some benefits he thought.

The main reception was nicely laid out with coloured plants at each corner. Huge wall coverings with biophilic design patterns in the most vibrant of colours that gave the place a lift. The natural wood reception desk and a lovely receptionist who always had a beaming smile to greet visitors and clients.

Philip loved the coloured flowers, but often wondered if the girl had access to the prescription cabinet and was maybe self-medicating. I mean how can she be so happy in a room filled with unhappy people? Philip noticed every time he arrived how brilliantly white her teeth are. Her teeth's brilliance extenuated by the wideness of her smile.

He wondered if she was perhaps bleaching her teeth to give the pearl white effect. Feeling conscientious, Philip pursed his lips tighter to keep his smoke and coffee stained enamels under wraps.

'May I help you?' she asks. Directing her question to the lady standing in front of Philip. Her accent is educated he thought to himself. Or perhaps coached is the more correct word. Not that he would be judgemental on an accent but guessed a receptionist duty requires a certain voice. Clarity of expression and politeness as pre-requisites for selection.

'Philip Burns?' calls the receptionist that is his prompt to raise his index finger to signal acknowledgement that he is here. 'They are ready for you now' she signals towards the next doors.

Passing through the waiting room and through the next doors into the consultation room. Nothing fancy. There was no competition here to come up with a design for therapy rooms. Battleship grey paint must have been sold in bulk at a discount price. Perhaps the blandness was all part of the therapeutic approach he wondered.

After a few minutes, a young lady enters the small box room

and sits across the table from Philip. Of course, they have met before and go through the normal pleasantries about the weather, the traffic, and the state of world politics. This is to enable the client to settle down or relax before the session formally begins.

'So, what would you like to talk about today?' is the opening line. This is accompanied by some head nodding gestures and a smile from both participants as they mirror reflect each other's behaviour. It is always best to sit upright, and Philip adjusts his pose accordingly.

'Well, since last week, I've been feeling a bit low. I think, you know, with the lockdown and social distancing, I have missed my friends and going out.'

'Ah yes, I know what you mean. Can you tell me more about that?'

After a slight reflective pause during which eyes focus away on the corner of the room. Philip notices these small behavioural patterns from experience.

'It's like every day is the same for me. Sometimes I wonder if I should just vanish and what would happen. Or would anyone actually notice I'm gone?'

There is a pause here in the conversation as notes are scribbled. Some more head nodding intended to draw the conversation deeper.

'That's interesting. Can you tell me more?'

This time, eyes drop to the fingernails and playing with the fingers as a distraction behaviour. Perhaps concealing nervousness about something about to be revealed. The room clock ticks away the seconds.

'I get so angry recently. Sometimes at the smallest of things. It does not take too much to push me over the edge. I just lose my temper and throw the nearest object.'

Philip notices from the corner of his eye that there is only 15 minutes left of the session They always finish on time.

'Interesting. Can you elaborate more on what losing your temper means and how does that make you feel?'

Philip feels a deep brain fog descend. It is a strange sensation. He knows that it is happening and that there is little that he can do about it except let it run through. When this happens, Philip's alter ego takes control. His mind wanders for a few minutes and then snaps back to reality.

'I am so sorry, looks like we have just run out of time' breaks the silence. 'Doesn't the time pass so quickly?' Philip's attention is brought back to the room and the moment as though stumbling on the last step.

'The receptionist will make a new appointment for next week' is the last voice spoken.

Back out through the waiting room, the pearl white teeth receptionist smiles as though someone has just made her day. What is she looking at? Philip thinks to himself as he stares back at her teeth filled smile.

She hands him a small card with a date and time filled in as she looks through him to attend to her next waiting client. As he turns away from the desk, he glances around at the poor souls waiting their turn. The solemn looks around the room are prevalent. No one acknowledges anyone. Instead eyes are down at the square tiled carpet floor.

On exit, there is some commotion behind that Philip ignores. Afterall, there is always some drama going on in these centres.

Taking his hands from his pockets he puts on his face mask and adjusts it so that it covers his nose and mouth. It gives him a feeling of anonymity. Fitting in with the crowd.

Time for a coffee before my next client Philip muses feeling a stress headache coming on.

Alice was the only other customer in the café, and she was busy making notes in her journal that she completely ignored Philip as he walked in. He gave a small hand gesture to her that she ignored.

Situational perspective is a crucial factor in influencing our emotional state. Familiarity with the setting may prompt a response of expectation. We see, hear, and feel what we expect in a familiar setting. Active engagement with others requires conscious effort to notice what is different and not make presumptions on what we expect to be.

Alice finished shorthand writing in her journal and closed her eyes again.

SEDATION

18 Weeks ago.

How can it be that he is gone? At least the man I married is gone. This man is just a shell of my husband, it feels as if he is a stranger. We are years together. First engaged and now ten years married. The highest and lowest moments of our life shared together. Of course, I still love him. At least in a way that married people do after so many years together if that counts as love any more.

My mother always told me that I had made my own bed to lie in and should stop complaining. Married couples got on with life and stayed together no matter what.

Perhaps we are destined to be where we are and my destiny, our destiny has brought us both to this point. But for a long time, things between us are not good. I wondered had I made a mistake building my life with this man. He seemed devoid of ambition and was content with living week to week. His lack of ambition just annoyed me so much sometimes.

But the last few months were different. Three months of lockdown followed by social distancing and travel restrictions meant that we saw no one except each other. And of course, the kids. This had an unforeseen toll on both of us. It felt like he was someone else. He had these strange stories to tell. He told me one time that he knew what was going to be said next on the television before it was said. Yep, how is anyone supposed to react to that? I asked him how that could be.

Of course, he did not answer, or perhaps could not. Instead just becoming secretive and quiet. Turning inwards to escape what was happening around him.

In his mind he was always right. It was obvious that there was more going on inside his mind than outside. For a long time, he could just sit staring into space as though watching a soap opera unravelling in his mind. He seemed content in this inner world that only he could see. I found it terrible of course, and worse when they came to take him away. He resisted fiercely and it broke my heart to watch him struggle pitifully.

Now he is in the psychiatric ward of the local hospital for a couple of weeks. He calls it the crazy house. I find it so difficult to visit him in that place. It drains my energy every time I go through the doors to visit him. But then, it also takes me out of my daily routine. He appears oblivious to the effort and distress that I must endure to get to him. Then to sit there for an hour in silence. No one speaking. Just the cries and screams in the background of other lost souls.

He is not himself anymore. And thinking back, probably not for a long time. First his strange behaviour that got more and more dangerous. One time, I arrived home from work to find all the windows and doors wide open in the house. It was the middle of winter! And not just that, the gas cooker was on full, with no pilot light, just gas pouring out. I could hear the gas escaping. I felt sick to my core. The entire house and everything in it could have just went up into the air with a puff of smoke. 'Everything must go' he shouted angrily in my face when I reached to shut the gas off.

Confused, he stared back at me with wild eyes bulging from his head. For the first time in my life, I was afraid of him. I did not recognise him anymore. I knew there was no reason for it. Maybe then I should have called the police or the ambulance. But I just could not. How could I let my own husband be locked up? It was like I had failed him or let him down in some way. But in the end, that is exactly what I did. Now, I am no longer afraid of him, but I also do not recognize him anymore. He walks around like a zombie. Pumped full of sedatives.

Before we got to this point, winter, spring, and summer had passed. Everyone warned me. 'This is not normal carry on. Look how he is behaving.'

'Send him to a doctor.'

I did ask him to go to the doctor, but he just would not go. He is an adult man; I cannot force him to do something he does not want.

But after the incident with the gas, I had no choice. I just did not trust him anymore with the children. Not that I thought he would deliberately do something to hurt anyone, but in his crazy moments, anything was possible. It was only time before he blew up the whole house. With the children inside.

I decided to go to the local doctor myself. I wanted to talk to someone, a professional, who could look at my situation objectively. I was always a strong person but the minute I stepped into the consultation room; I just broke down. The tears streamed down my face and for minutes I just could not speak. I could not get a word passed my lips. The doctor passed me the tissues and gave me a glass of water.

With starts and stops, I told him the whole story.

'You don't have two, but three children' he said.

I pulled my eyebrows up. I felt understood. Later I realised that the doctor was right. My husband was no longer a fully functioning adult. I just could not rely on him anymore. And yet felt obligated to look after him.

A cold wind took the autumn leaves off the trees when I got a telephone call from the police. Asking if I could collect the dog from the station. They had picked up Frank walking down a section of the motorway close by our house. He was walking the dog. It was a life saver that they had found him when they did. It could have turned out so different that day. I went to the station and found him sitting in a cell. The door was open, so some consolation. I collected the dog and the ambulance collected Frank. He was a danger to himself and others around him. But he was assessed not crazy enough to be held for long. After a couple of days, Frank arrived home by taxi.

'They had no white bread' was the only words he spoke as he walked through the front door. He did not speak again after that for four days and then only responded when he wanted me to get something for him.

There was nothing else to do except wait until he would go off the rails again. It did not take long. After work, I had collected the children from school and just arrived home when I heard a commotion outside from down the end of our street. A strange calmness came over me. I was quiet, clear headed and decisive. I knew exactly what needed to be done. I brought the children to one of the neighbours and called the emergency services.

After three months or so, life is slowly returning to some normality for me. I am back working at the hospital and feel back in control of my life. Once I knew Frank was safely locked up and getting his treatment, I was content and ready to move on with my life. My work took up my days and kept me occupied. As I turn back to my next patient, I look up to see Frank's familiar eyes now devoid of emotion or awareness. I rubbed the alcohol wipe across his bare arm and inserted the syringe to deliver his daily dose of sedative.

I felt safe again and smiled.

Alice Braithward looked at her own reflection in the cross wired glass of the visiting room. She looked old she thought to herself.

Ignoring obvious signals of mental distress in someone you know, hoping that it will go away may result in circumstance that are irrecoverable for everyone involved. She mused.

Alice picked up the EEG scans for Franks brainwave patterns and noted the low alpha power signals as an indication of neurocognitive decline.

There was no coming back for this man she concluded.

EXPIRED LOVE

16 Weeks ago.

This never happens. Most nights he is downstairs for hours on end watching news programs about race riots in a different country or continent. Or he is often not at home at all. An urgent business meeting or 'business need' to be taken care of. Sometimes, he must conveniently meet his friends down the local to clear his head. She lay in the king size bed, completely alone. No one to snuggle up to. No one to hug. No one. It felt like he was avoiding her, as though he did not want to be close to her. She had never imagined her marriage to be like this. She thought that a husband always wanted his wife and that the wife should always be available for his needs. She thought that her husband would every moment want to be with her. And there were times in the past when he could not stay away from her and every free moment, they spent with each other. Lately though, she wore pyjamas to bed.

She knew that there was a growing distance between them but could not explain why. She just wanted to feel his presence again. Not just his empty shell in the house but his entire presence as though he wanted to be here. She wanted to be wrapped in his arms. The strength and security in his strong embrace. She wanted him back and would do anything to make sure that happened. She also felt the smallest of dents in her self-confidence. She was not sure if it was already too late to turn her marriage around.

As though in a trance, he stares at the television. He has more interest in his programs than he does in her. She lay awake half the night. She felt not just alone but also lonely. She missed him, even when he was in the same room. She decided to bring up the conversation yet again. And not for the first time.

'About last night, why are you avoiding me?'

'Did I? I wasn't aware that I was avoiding you, I have work to think about.'

She felt her anger rise inside her at his dismissive tone. Dumbass she says in her mind.

'Yes, come on, you stay up all night watching the television news channels. You push me away from you if I come close to snuggle up beside you.'

'I was tired.' He responded without turning from the television.

'I understand your tired after work, but you never plan anytime for us to do something special even on your days off from work.'

'I don't have the energy to do anything special' he responds curtly.

Her eyes grow wider. 'But I do!'

'I can't do anything about that.'

What an egotistical control freak. It is like everything must turn around what he wants.

'There is no man in the world that just sits and wants to watch television the whole time when at home.'

'Sure....'

Nothing else comes out of his mouth. The penny has still not dropped. He should be doing more to make her happy and not only think of himself.

'Are you not attracted to me anymore?' she asks.

'Of course.'

'How come then I don't feel that? I don't think that you are.'

Slowly, his eyes turn from the television to hers.

'I don't know.' Shrugging his shoulders. She sighs loudly.

'I think that you have changed,' he says.

'I have changed?!' She blurts out her anger rising inside.

'Yes. Before you used to laugh a lot. I found that nice about you. But that girl is not you anymore.'

'You give me no reason to laugh, hah!' To her, the conversation was already lost at this point.

'So now it's my fault?' He crosses his arms over each other.

'No. Yes. I do not know. You also changed,' she says.

'How am I changed?'

'We are both changed. We are both older and we have experienced a lot together in the last few years.'

'I don't hear how I've changed. Give me a real example?'

'I think it's terrible that you have pushed me away as I got older. Did you expect I'd always be 21?'

'I don't expect that at all. I just want you to laugh more.'

'That all depends on when I don't come home anymore' she says.

'I get it. Do not be so unreasonable. You understand what I mean.'.

'Yeah, you don't find me funny anymore.'

He waves his arm to dismiss the conversation and turns his attention back to the television. He says nothing more.

She must get out of here. Her thoughts spinning in her head. If she stays at home, then it will turn into a full-blown argument. And she does not want that. At least the dog is happy that things are not going so well between them. The black Labrador wags its tail with excitement. She picks up the dog's lead and it jumps enthusiastically, expectant of what comes next. At least someone is happy to be with her. It is going to be a long walk. She must get her head calm.

Is he right? Perhaps she is too negative and does not give him the space he needs for himself. Afterall, no one comes home happy to a nagging wife and she realises that she has not been a happy person for a long time. She wants to change that, be happy again. But perhaps she can't – is it already too late – already too old? She is not the fun girl anymore that she once was. He has said it a few times and of course he knows me best. The black dog was pulling strong tonight as it led her away from the lights towards the railway track.

The dark clouds filled her mind on that last walk many years ago.

There are few visitors anymore. Time heals and memory fades. The husband kneels to his wife's graveside placing the token bunch of flowers against the headstone. They will not last long though. Nothing survives a lack of love.

The husband looks up to see the presence of an older woman. She looks well into her eighties and holding a walking stick to support her.

'I'm sorry for your loss' she says looking sadly down on the bereaved man.

'Thank you. We are all still in shock. I do not even know how it happened that night. We never owned a dog, so I do not know why people said they saw her walking a black dog. Or how could she have? Or how did she get to where she was?' So many unanswered questions that will never be answered.

Alice turned to walk away thinking to herself how depression is becoming more and more common. Perhaps as people are more aware of the symptoms and a societal acceptance of depression as a mental health issue. The 'black dog' analogy is symbolic of depression and gives those who are prone to the symptoms a way to verbalise a mental health condition perhaps reducing the stigma associated with the term 'depression.

ATTENTION DEFICIT

The non-stop flight from London to San Francisco was already well under way. Louise and Jeff who were already seated up front beside each other like to share a bag of Iced Caramel Sweets on the journey. His favourite of course. And he gobbles them down so quickly that Louise wondered if he was trying to induce sugar intolerance or just loose his teeth prematurely.

Of course, Louise was just partaking out of courtesy. His best activity on a long-haul flight was sleeping. For Louise, she would pass the time watching the small screens in front of her while listening to her favourite music. She might also take in an audio book for an hour or two. The more fantastic, the more non-believable, the better. She just loved fantasy fiction stuff. As an alternative she might select some obscure audio program about gardening. Anyway, either audio option distracted her mind just enough to let the travel time pass without being too taxing on the mind.

Jeff prattled on about how tired he was after his hectic weekend. He went on about some football match that he was watching last night. Louise pretended to listen as she really had no interest in football. This was their normal conversation banter that made Louise think that perhaps their partnership was more one of convenience instead of any mutual respect or interest for each other. Still, the relationship did have some benefits of course. He was still pleasing on the eye. He kept himself well groomed for a man she thought, glancing to her side to look Jeff up and down. Although his choice of aftershave was cheap, she concluded harshly.

The flight progress map indicated the flight passing to the south of Iceland and heading on towards Greenland. A busy flight with very few spare seats. There was a lot of young children on the plane but since it was already two hours into the flight they had calmed down by now and the many portable game console screens fluttered every now and then around the passenger cabin.

The lighting had already started to dim in the cabin as passengers started to progressively close the window shutters in preparation for travel sleep. All appeared to be right with the world as the plane cruised high above the frozen landscape below.

There was an elderly woman on the flight that night that appeared to be having some difficulty with her breathing. Approaching the coast of Greenland, the cabin crew make a request announcement for any nurse or doctor to make themselves known to a member of cabin crew. Neither Louise nor Jeff really batted an eye at this announcement.

As seasoned transatlantic travellers, this was not something new to them. And so, Louise continued to watch and listen to her program and Jeff continued to doze in and out of sleep covered in a blanket of crinkly sweet wrappers and pieces of crystalised sugar. Some people enjoy travel more than others she surmised to herself.

In his moments of sleep, Jeff appeared to be jumping and fidgeting in his sleep as though dreaming. This did not raise any concerns for his partner. She looked on at him and wondered how it is that some people can sleep anywhere.

The flight navigational tracking map was the first indication that the flight was deviating from flight path. Louise noticed it first on the overhead screen in front of her and nudged Jeff to tell him the news. Jeff muttered something back about high blood sugar levels, stomach cramps and never eating another iced caramel.

His recent bouts of fatigue were annoying sometimes and not conducive to a good conversation or just keeping your partner engaged on a long trip.

'Look!' exclaimed Louise followed by another elbow jab to

Jeff's side.

'We are veering slightly to the right'.

Certainly, the plane could be felt to be gently leaning towards the right wing. But it was a gradual turn and not something that would by itself raise any concerns.

Jeff wiped the sleep from his eyes as he focused on the small digital screen mounted on the bulkhead in front of them.

'There is a strong weather storm in front' said Jeff assuredly as he turned awkwardly in his seat trying to find his comfort position. Louise thought Jeff is probably right returning to the screen in front of her. Afterall, he does think he knows everything she mused.

After another fifteen minutes flying, Louise looked up and noticed that the flight progress map was flickering. Glancing at Jeff, his eyes had closed again and was making strange breathing noises as he alternately breathed through his mouth that made a noise like a horse when he exhaled. She turned her attention back to the display screen adjusting her headphone set for comfort. Just as she did, she noticed a vibration coming through the floor of the craft that she could feel on the soles of her feet. Readjusting her seat position to place her feet flat on the floor – yes there it was. She was sure. The small passenger tv screens paused as the seatbelt warning chimed and the cabin crew made the announcement to fasten seatbelts.

The vibration of the aircraft became progressively worse and the plane banked sideways making a hard turn. Louise grabbed hold of her arm rests to pull herself upright in the seat. She tried in vain to correct the turn extending her left and then right leg. Throughout the passenger cabin, passengers made nervous sounds as the clicking of seat belts could be heard over the sound of the engine surges. A sudden altitude decrease caused ears to pop as the plane descended to a lower altitude. Oxygen masks dropped from the bulkhead overhead.

'Jeff, Jeff, what is happening?' she called out.

He was now sitting upright and fully alert but there was no response. He appeared momentarily dazed as though not sure of his surroundings.

Time appeared to stand still over the next minutes. The plane banked left and then right struggling to maintain altitude. The crew struggled to maintain control of the aircraft through heavy vibration and cross winds.

'Reduce flaps 10%'

'Confirmed'. Increase engine throttle 20% left side'.

'Hold steady. Hold it steady'. Maintain air speed'.

The plane descended rapidly through cloud cover and began to level off as the plane lined up for the unscheduled runway visit to Baffin Island just inside the arctic circle. It is not an easy one as this airport does not usually get visits from large commercial aircraft. The plane makes several circles of the airport before final approach burning off as much fuel weight as possible. The clunk of landing gear locking into place is the final indication of an attempted runway approach.

Touch down is hard. There is gasps and nervous exclamations from the passengers that signal relief. Brakes applied hard create a screeching noise as the plane begins to decrease its trajectory down the small single lane runway.

Finally, the plane comes to a shuddering stop at the furthest end of the icy runway. Momentarily, the plane rocks forwards and backwards on its compressed suspension as though teetering on the edge of some precipice before finally stopping. Louise looked out across the icy expanse before them but took consolation that, at least for now, that the plane was stopped.

From her side window, she could see the red flashing lights of the ground emergency services arriving beside the plane and took some comfort from that. The instruction to evacuate the plane was given. Turning to look over her shoulder, she could see the crew force opening the cabin doors behind her and rolling out the evacuation chutes as more emergency vehicles surrounded the vehicle.

Louise quickly adjusted her headphone set. Looking across at Jeff beside her, he was dazed but was moving and was uninjured as far as she could make out. 'We need to evacuate the plane Captain' he spoke as he quickly started to unbuckle his belt to release himself from the seat.

'Yes – do it now. I will follow you out' said Louise in a clam tone.

DECEASED

I guess, like many others, I am uncomfortable at funerals. What to wear, what to say, who should I say it to, goes on in my mind the day before that drives me bonkers. The news of the passing of Mark's father was not exactly a surprise. I did not know his father so had no expectation either way. Mark on the other hand, I have known for many years. Although I have never heard mention of his Father before his short illness and ultimate demise. I reckoned that I should attend the funeral to show support. To express condolences to an old friend in the passing of his Dad. At least, that is what I told myself.

I heard through our friends' group chat that the body was going to be 'waked' in the family house on the Wednesday night and the funeral on the following morning. The plan was communicated via the WhatsApp group and the options outlined. Attend at the wake on Wednesday night, or attend the 'full on' funeral the following day. Ok. Makes sense to get it over with as quickly as possible and avoids taking a day off work to attend the funeral of someone I do not even know.

The following night, I made my way down to the small terrace house lit up with every light on and cars parked all over the small street. The front door was wide open and there was a lot of people mulling around outside smoking. Others outside were passive smoking out of ignorance. The hallway into the house was similarly jammers with people on either side of the narrow hallway meaning you had to scrunch your way through with repeated apologies.

'Excuse me. Sorry. Excuse me. So Sorry' was the password to

get through chatting bystanders.

Eventually, I got to the central command station. Also known as the Kitchen. I caught my old friends' eye, and he made a bee line straight for me through the dark suits. It surprised me that he would have the thought to even come over to me in the circumstances.

'Thanks for coming' he said placing his hand onto my arm turning me towards the next door. 'He's laid out in the next room if you wanted to see him?' continued Mark.

I did not really want to see a dead body of someone I had never met before. But it was too late. I was ushered into the small front living room. The room was tiny. The coffin had to be placed diagonal in the centre of the room directly under the wall mounted 52-inch flat screen TV.

'Come on, I'll introduce you' Mark blurted out with enthusiasm.

I snatched my arm back from the being led position. 'Ah sure your grand Mark, I don't want to disturb your Dad' I blurted out. I know. I know that makes no sense. His Dad is not going to be disturbed at this stage.

'Don't be silly, you are here now. 'Dad look who's come to see you' shouted Mark at his father. Maybe he was hard of hearing I wondered when he was alive that carried forward in death

Of course, there was no response from the father. He did not move. Just very serious looking as though... well, as though he was dead.

'Doesn't he look well?' continued Mark, this time addressing the question to me.

'Ah, yeah he does. Lovely suit. Hard to believe he is gone'. I rattled off without too much thinking.

'And his life friend Brenda is going with him, isn't she Dad?' said Mark to his deceased father.' The old girl was with him for years. Looking after him every day while he was sick. At least they stayed together. They couldn't be separated in life or death.'

I felt my eyes widen as if by automatic reflex as I stared at my friend leaning over his father's coffin, gently stroking his father's head. I instinctively drew closer to the side of the coffin and my friend. It was one body in the coffin I confirmed.

My mind processed the scene around me and what I had just heard spoken. The lavender wallpaper of the small front room taunted my mind. A discoloured picture on the mantlepiece of a happy couple. Presumably, Mark's mum and dad in times long past. With the curtains closed and the lights on, it created a yellowish artificial glow of everything. The giant oversized flat screen created a mirrored reflection of the surreal scene. My mind played tricks on me, I thought I saw the reflection of an older woman looking back from the mirror. She appeared to be laughing as she watched the scene.

His best friend is going with him! I said in my mind without speaking the words.

'Where is she laid out?' I asked gently. Tipping my head to one side and nodding at the same time.

Mark turned to look at me square on. 'She's in her own box of course' he confirmed.

'I'm sorry, I didn't realise it was a double wake'.

'Do you want to see her?' Mark asked.

'No, you're alright, thanks' I blurted out quickly.

'That is terrible. I am so sorry. I didn't realise that your mother was gone as well.'

Mark looked back at me with a confused look on his face. 'My mother is in the Kitchen' he said.

At this point I just wanted to leave. There is only so much bereavement that one can take.

Mark reached down into his Dad's coffin and withdrew a small boxed object. 'Here she is' he exclaimed offering the small square pine box towards me. It was no bigger than a cigar box and had a small inscription on the top. 'In life together, but forever in death'.

'We had her cremated when she died and got permission from the church to bury her with my Dad'.

Some other mourners were entering the small front room to pay their respects. I realised that there was a queue forming behind us. I was glad of the interruption. I carefully handed back the small cremation box and squeezed myself out of the tiny room and back into the kitchen hoping to find the exit.

Mark's younger sister approached. 'Thanks for coming. Mark will be glad you are here' she ventured gently leaning into me. 'No problem' I said patting her on the shoulder.

Same as her brother, she caught my arm and pulled me forward to introduce me to her mother. This woman was certainly alive and sitting upright on one of those hard kitchen chairs. She held a tissue in her hand and frequently dabbed her face. Yep, I thought, she is alive.

'So sorry for your loss' I offered as I bent forward and shook her hand. What a strange custom I thought. She nodded as though hearing the platitude for at least a hundred times already. Sure, what else does someone say?

'He's gone to a better place' she said as I stood upright. I wondered where she could be referring to but decided not to open that discussion.

'His mind was going anyway. There was many a day that he would say, I will bring the dog for a walk and go out the front door forgetting to bring the old mutt back with him. I think they were almost as mad as each other. At least he has not forgotten to take the dog with him this time!'

Mark's sister had already left me and was tending to other mourners. I mulled around and decided I would make my way back out to the front door for air and space. This entailed passing back down the narrow hallway past the awkward queue of mourners forming against one side of hall as though an unofficial traffic management system. A couple of nods and I was out in fresh air.

For a moment I thought I could hear the barking of a small Jack Russel somewhere in the distance and felt an odd sensation as though someone was watching me.

TRANSIENT MEMORY

Alan was a carpenter living in London with his wife of twenty years. Like many men of his generation, he was a creature of habit. His daily routine was to have breakfast with his wife Julie, then a quick shower followed by a walk around a four-mile loop near where they lived.

Alan enjoyed his walk. He saw it as his time and would reflect on yesterday and plan ahead for the workday.

The previous day was slightly different than his usual. While finishing off an office fit out job for a commercial client, he saw a notice board advert looking for trial volunteers to conduct an experiment in relaxation and brain signals.

Handy money he thought for thirty minutes listening to some background music. So, he readily signed up.

The event was, well, disappointingly mundane. He did not take the time to read the information leaflet and did not really understand what the trial was about. All he knew was that it would make you relax.

In reality, Time Shift was running trials on behalf of an undersea sonar mapping company that used ULF signals to map the seabed. There was some tentative evidence suggesting a connection between recent Whale and Dolphin beaching in the area and the sonar mapping.

Low frequency signals carry easily through water and could theoretically effect mammals such as Whales and Dolphins that use their own sonar to navigate. Since it was not possible to create the tests on sea mammals, the next closest mammal was human.

After his thirty-minute trial, Alan drove home that evening relaxed and refreshed. Pleased with himself and an extra £10 in his pocket.

The next morning, Alan followed his normal daily routine. He did his walk, went to work and nothing seemed amiss until he got home later that evening.

'What time is it?' he asked Julie as he sat down at the Kitchen table.

'It's 8:30 pm' she replied glancing at the large kitchen clock.

After a short pause of about a minute, Alan asked the question again. 'What time is it?'

Julie assumed he had not heard her the first time and responded, 'It's still 8:30!'

'But what time is it now?'

Julie turned to face her husband, annoyed, as he sat at their kitchen table staring into space. Here was another example of him not listening she thought to herself.

'Are you going deaf or deliberately not listening to me?' she asked.

Alan seemed expressionless. She looked closer at his face that was motionless except for the blinking of an eye.

'What time is it?' he spoke again.

'What is wrong with you?' she asked out of a growing annoyance with Alan's behaviour. 'Are you teasing me or trying to be funny because I'm not laughing' she said.

'What time is it?' repeated Alan.

'Ok, that's enough of the game playing. I'm not interested anymore and your starting to worry me now' raising her voice, changing from annoyance to fear.

Julie sat down beside Alan and in her heart knew that something was not right. His eyes were motionless staring away into space. His face looked rigid and fixed in time.

'What time is it?' repeated Alan.

'Alan. Are you ok?' with worry in her tone she clasped his hand in hers.

With panic growing, she led Alan by the hand from the Kitchen to the living room. His walk was normal, his faced was not drooping, he followed her lead easily as she sat Alan down on the couch. 'Alan, it's me Julie.

Are you ok?'

Alan momentarily turned and looked at his wife without registering recognition or any other emotion. 'What time is it?' he asked again.

Sometime later, the emergency paramedic team arrived at the door of the house. Julie was highly agitated at this stage as she opened the door to the paramedics with tears streaming down her face. The paramedics found him in a part catatonic state and immediately brought him to the local hospital suspecting a stroke. On admittance, Alan was led by hand through the ward and into the consultant's examination room. Julie's distress did not register with Alan and his face remained emotionless, devoid of feeling or recognition for her. He seemed completely unaware of his surroundings and what was happening to him.

By now, some two hours had passed since Alan's initial event. He kept repeating the same question over and over but now started to add a new question. 'Where am I?'

He repeated this question over and over and occasionally reverted to 'what time is it?'

Neurological scans showed unusual low frequency brain wave activity across his frontal lobes and the signal frequency was erratic. Alan's memory centres also appeared quiet. All other functions appeared to be normal. He could hear and see. The tone, power and coordination of his limbs were as they should be. His reflexes appeared all normal and his toes turned down when the consultant scratched the sole of his feet. His behaviour was that of a child and he would take the hand of anyone that offered it.

Willing to be led in any direction as though a child separated from its parents lost in a supermarket.

About an hour later, Alan suddenly piped up and asked, 'What are you all doing?' His facial expression changed, and he smiled as he once again recognized his wife sitting beside him holding his hand still in hers. Gone was the robotic motionless expressions and he drew a smile across his face. 'What are we doing here?' he asked. This time turning and looking around at the anxious faces staring back at him.

'I'm fine Julie,' with a laugh in his tone. 'Has something happened to you – why are we at the hospital?' he continued seemingly oblivious to how he had arrived here.

Alan's last memory was some ten hours ago when he recollected having breakfast with his wife. He had no recollection of his morning walk or of being at work earlier that day. Subsequent electrical magnetic scans of the brain all showed normal function. His blood tests all returned fine with no abnormality. Except for a missing ten hours of memory loss that Alan would never recall, his recovery appeared complete.

Alan subsequently returned to working on building sites as a carpenter and went about his job as normal. There was no relapses and monthly check-ups soon lapsed to quarterly and eventually annually before stopping completely. However, his work colleges reported that Alan's personality had changed. He became less conscientious about his work, ignored safe working practices, and subsequently took to excessive alcohol consumption.

Julie on the other hand experienced a shock that she could not forget. Her experience terrified her as her life partner had suddenly disappeared. She expressed how her feelings towards life changed and recognized the transient and fragile nature of life. She described her feelings of horror as she and her husband cruised through their existence together like many others with ordinary hopes and fears that had suddenly disappeared that day. Her husband replaced by a lost and confused child for a day.

Unlike Alan, Julie was unable to recover and revert to some normal continuation of life. She held a deep-seated fear of a repeat occurrence that affected her badly. This fear expressed itself though sleeplessness, anxiety and ultimately depression.

Alan and Julie separated some years after the event and went on to lead their own separate lives.

Time Shift Inc decided not to publish the trial results. But presumably, they got the answer that they wanted.

CYCLE OF TIME

12 Weeks ago.

James had always had an interest in technical toys. Especially old ones. Since his retirement from a few years ago he had developed an interest in vintage bicycles and much to the annoyance of his wife, spent a lot of his meagre pension, on purchasing and restoration. It was not a business per se. If the definition of a business is making money, then this was a hobby. James felt that working with old bikes gave him some yearned for connection to the past.

Part of this hobby excitement for James was visiting salvage yards and house sales looking for the bicycle that could be bought cheap enough. And just as importantly, can be repaired within the limitations of James technical skills and his toolbox. This was one of those days. James had taken the old van and travelled out to an estate sale where the contents of an old house were going to be sold off. There was a reference in the sale brochure of bicycles and parts that James thought could be interesting.

Some background checks, mainly through google, suggested the house was from late 19th Century and occupied until the 1980's until the owner had died. A disputed will had the property in probate for a number of years thereafter and local authority dereliction notices issued in the 90's ensured that any residual value in the property was long gone. Still, this is where James sought opportunity in his little hobby venture.

The estate sale was busy. This disappointed James. He was not fond of crowds as they often forced higher prices. The first couple of lots were nominated sales as dealers snapped up catalogued items of art and restoration furniture. China plates and cutlery were similarly gobbled up by the professional bidders. They were worth a watch though as they performed the most elaborate behaviours to hide their bid interest from competitors. Nods and winks, super quick waving of a hand, the scratch. All signals to the auctioneer podium of an interest bid. James decided to keep his hands in his pockets during this part of the sale for fear he would end up with a purchase of a carpet or perhaps some chandelier.

James's target purchase was the very last lot of the day. Looking around the sale room, the serious buyers had already departed and there was a queue to settle at the auctioneer's payment booth.

'Final lot of the day. No reserve. The delivery bicycle and associated parts from circa 1963. Thought to have been owned by the lady of the house, this bicycle needs a loving home.' The auctioneer prattled on from his podium. He continued for another minute as he made some flamboyant gestures with his hands trying to get the lot sold. James waited and then raised his hand to place his bid at the chosen time.

A bit more auctioneer prattle and the hammer clacked sold. James had what he came for.

It was another hour before James finally turned onto his driveway in his van. I will get it unloaded now into the garage and sort it out tomorrow he thought. Margaret, his wife, came to the door and strolled out to the back of the van.

'Another load of rubbish, I suppose'. She doled out.

However, James was used to this greeting and knew best to ignore and just get the van unloaded into the garage as quickly as possible. Margaret hated having the old van on the driveway. She said it gave the neighbours a bad impression. Like perhaps they were poor or something.

Van unloaded and parked away down the side out of view of anyone. James looked forward to unpacking his box the following day.

'Where is the Stanley Knife?' roared James the following morning up the stairs to Margaret. She shouted back her normal response as though familiar to the question.

'Where you left it last time dear.'

This infuriated James that he cursed his wife under his breath. He grabbed the best kitchen knife, stormed out to his garage hide-away and started dismantling the cardboard boxed contents.

The old bicycle was sort of a disappointment. It was a black green rust colour with tired wheels and saddle. James gingerly stood the machine upright and started to wipe down the years of grime from the cycle component parts. The wheels and chain were at least free to turn although the tyres had long since perished. James decided to get out his notebook and make a list of jobs needed. This was his way. A throw back to his working career days. If it is worth doing, it is worth doing right, he muttered under his breath.

Two weeks later, and the box of parts had arrived courtesy of e-bay and the postman. James was out in the garage assembling the components and checking them off his 'master list'. The Project was proceeding to plan. The original saddle was unusual. It was leather covered and had an unusual arrangement of polished springs that gave it great support. James marvelled at its construction and assembly and decided it was a piece of craftmanship from a bygone era. He carefully cleaned the leather seat and reinstalled it on the seat post. 'Marvellous' he exclaimed. A final spin of the newly refurbished chain and the spoked wheels rotated with a click sound that you might hear from an old swiss time piece. At least in James's mind.

After a final height adjustment, James wheeled the bicycle out to the front of the house and the roadway. With a leg over he was away. His mind worked though his checklist a final time.

Brakes work – check. Steering works – check. Pedals work – check.

Pushing the pedals, a bit harder, the bike meandered its way down the road. The saddle was supremely comfortable thought James. Cannot beat the originals he thought to himself. Don't know where the modern plastic saddles came from. A passing car whizzed past a bit too fast and too close for comfort. It forced James to readjust his cycling position and move closer to the road edge. Carefully through the next junction, James wanted to avoid traffic. Cars and bicycles simply do not mix. He was starting to settle now and complimented himself on getting the old bike back up and running. He wondered who the last person before him was to sit in this saddle.

At least on the smaller roads there was less car traffic. James was nearing his turn around point at the next bend just before the old schoolhouse, when a truck came from the other direction. The last thing that James remembered was the orange colour of the truck cab and the wide truck mirrors. When he opened his eyes next, he could see the blue of the sky as he looked up from the roadway. There was no sound. There was no pain or discomfort. Just a blue sky with small wisps of clouds passing in between the blueness. James felt a heaviness come over him as he closed his eyes.

Sometime later, James re opened his eyes but to a different scene. He was aware of lots of people around him. A part familiar voice called his name. Initially it sounded in the distance but steadily drew closer and clearer.

'James, James, can you hear me?'

James blinked to focus his eyes. He could see the blurred outline of others around him.

'Where am I?' he blurted out.

His voice was drowned out by the sound of young children playing. As James looked towards the sound, he could see children at play in the school yard. They ran and jumped, shouting, and hollering. Running around each other in uniforms of grey and red that blended as they rushed around the walled in space. James instantly recognized the old school. It was where he had attended many years ago. He recognized the uniform with a warm familiarity of youth. For a moment, he thought he heard his old schoolteacher, Mrs O'Byrne, call his name.

'James! Get back inside the gate now.' She roared over the noise of play.

James felt the fear of reprimand like he had done many years ago during his formative years as a child. This cannot be right he thought to himself. The school closed more than forty years ago. Mrs O'Byrne's voice rang again in his ear.

'James! Are you deaf? Get in here now.' She roared into his face causing James to cower at the sound and wipe the spital from his cheeks.

James's mind told him he was at school. He felt the weight on his shoulder from the satchel strap and his knee length socks that irritated his skin on rainy days.

In T minus fifteen minutes, James would breathe for the last time.

James looked around the classroom and recognized the faces of some of his school friends from a long time ago. The wall calendar showed the year 1963. The large white-faced clock on the wall showed quarter to three. James recalled that school finished at 3 pm and wondered if his deceased mother was outside the gate waiting for him like she had done many years ago. Wait, there is something wrong here. This cannot be right.

T minus ten minutes.

A sudden sharp pain struck James across his face. Blinking, he looked to see Mrs O'Byrne's eyes looking back at him. Her hand drew back again, and James felt a second crack across his cheek. 'Answer the question Master James!' she roared into his reddened face.

T minus five minutes.

A firing of neurons in James brain caused pre-frontal cortex activity visible on the monitors. It looked as though a storm in the distance registering on a radar. Different memory centres fired randomly across both hemispheres. The superior olivary cortex registered and triggered a deep brain response. James's consciousness, his higher brain activity, started to take control.

'Wait. I think he's responding.'

'James, can you hear me? Open your eyes for us if you can.'

'Wait. Wait for my count before the next pulse signal shouted the doctor to her team'

'In three, two, one. Now'.

James blinked his eyes into alternate consciousness to see the square recessed lighting panels glare overhead. Inside, behind the outer glass diffuser, the small tube element flickered at a speed not detectable by human eyes. It gave the illusion of constant light. He felt drawn towards it.

Glimpse thoughts ran through his mind of times long past as though images on a carousel. He watched them flick by in his mind's eye. Overhead the light got brighter. Drawing him closer. James felt himself float above his body and looked down on the scene below him. He could make out the name tag of the Doctor who had worked his limp body so hard. He read Doctor Susan O'Byrne and thought of the coincidence of having a teacher and a doctor of the same last name. He saw the doctors team cease their efforts and stand back from his bedside.

And his wife holding her hands across her mouth as if to hold the sound from escaping.

James felt a squeeze of his hand.

'He is gone' said the Doctor. 'Time of Death 3:01 pm.'

ANGEL SIBLINGS

Jackie was late for our meeting and turned up looking a little flustered. This annoyed me but I decided that I will let this tardiness moment slide. Although I had not seen her for a long time, Jackie had a look of bohemian about her and I had an immediate impression that she shopped in vintage clothing stores. Although I had not seen her for many years, she made an impression on me straight away. She was in her mid-thirties and had developed a fixation or self-belief that she was losing the strength in her right hand.

Jackie explained that the problem with her right hand appeared over a period of time. She worked, or had worked, as a graphic designer and was right hand dominant. She said that she felt the strength in her hand diminish and became more and more prone to dropping things getting progressively worse over the last six months. I asked why it had taken her so long to get help. She hesitated to drop her eyes down to the left and said that she did not think it was anything serious.

Jackie had no other medical history to speak of and appeared in overall good health. However, she could not give any family medical history. She explained in a low whisper, that she has not had contact with her siblings for a long time now. Both parents were long deceased.

It is becoming more common that families fall into a dispute that can drag on for many years. This can result in siblings not talking to each other for many years or perhaps never. Often, they cannot remember how the original dispute started and instead perpetuate the disagreement out of a false sense of pride.

I asked Jackie if she would like to talk about her family. She paused again and I heard her take a deep breath. Her gaze once again moved down to the left before she looked me straight on.

'No. I prefer to not discuss it.'

On cursory examination, I could find nothing wrong with Jackie's hand. The tone, strength and co-ordination of her hand seemed to be normal. All reflexes appeared to be fine. As I went through my checklist, I asked Jackie what she had googled before coming to see me this morning.

'I never use the Internet. I find it such a waste of time and infiltrated with fake news stories.'

Although a strange response, it was a credible answer that I could certainly empathise with. However, for the third time, I noticed that Jackie threw her eyes down slightly towards the left. I realised that she was looking down at her left hand resting on her leg which appeared to tremor as she gazed at it.

'Jackie, can I ask if there is a reason that you look down to your left hand before speaking?'

She flinched at the question and I noticed her eyes widen as she stared back at me.

'I don't know what you're talking about' she said in a matter of fact tone. I felt as if I had touched a nerve and she was visibly agitated.

It crossed my mind that the hand tremor could be stress induced. I asked Jackie if there was any situation going on in her life that could be creating stress for her.

Once again, she dropped her eyes to her left hand, this time blushing slightly. I could now see the fingers on her left-hand tremoring slightly. The tips of her fingers spread wide and the hand appeared to be going through a stretch exercise as though trying to catch and hold air.

'No. I'm not under any stress. Aside from the family situation. I just do not like to speak about my parents or my siblings. I have a brother who only speaks to me on special occasions but never as a sister and never has time to answer my messages. He escaped home when he was sixteen or seventeen and left me with the mess of looking after our parents.'

'Well, I hope that the situation can be resolved, and perhaps we can discuss again.' I said.

Jackie took my prompt and stood up from her chair as if to leave. I reciprocated and stood to my feet. Jackie looked towards her left hand and raised it to her ear as though listening to her hand. I watched with anticipation of an explanation, but none was forthcoming.

I watched fascinated as Jackie put her jacket on, and her hand rose to 'speak' to her. I heard her whisper under her breath as though making conversation with some invisible force.

'I have to ask Jackie, are you talking to your hand?'

'Don't be silly' she said as she raised her left hand showing me the palm of her hand. 'This is my guardian angel.'

On the offer of a coffee, I persuaded Jackie to sit down again and tell me about her angel. She told me that over the last six months that her hand had taken on a life of its own and gave her advice on all aspects of life. It had become her guardian angel that she consulted with on a regular basis before any big decision. In a way, it gave her comfort and helped her to cope with anxiety and worry. At this point, she started to cry and caressed her left hand with her right as though stroking an invisible pet.

She explained that her father who was an abusive alcoholic, had left the family home when Jackie was still quiet young. Her mother had brought her up with her two younger brothers under difficult and financially stretched circumstances before passing away herself a few years ago after contracting pneumonia. Jackie explained how her father had turned up at her apartment last December after an absence of fifteen years. He was now wheelchair bound and hoped for care support from Jackie having received a diagnosis of neural dementia exacerbated by many years of excess alcohol and prescription drug abuse.

During the unwanted Christmas visit, Jackie had taken her father out to a nearby cliff side. While pointing the chair in the direction of the sea, she let loose of the chair and watched her father disappear over the cliff edge. She explained that her angel had given her instructions through her left hand.

As I sat opposite Jackie and listened to her story with amazement. But not surprise. Her hand tremor and the adoption of her limb as an 'angel' was strange but did not seem to present harm to her. If anything, it provided some comfort.

As she told me more about the abusive family situation, I felt a deep empathy for her actions. The abusive homelife resonated with me and I felt sorry for Jackie. I reached towards her and stroked her left hand.

'You did the right thing Jackie. Our mother would be proud.'

We both left that meeting with a new understanding for each other and resolved to stay in touch going forward as brother and sister should.

ALICE BRAITHWARD (NEE KELLY)

Alice Kelly had followed the emigration trail from rural Ireland to England to become a school cleaner. She had great aspirations to be more. But for now, this put food on the table. However, she had a strong sense that she came from a background of regrets and disappointments and she carried this belief around inside her. Ultimately, this belief choked her inside and prevented her from achieving her life ambitions.

Alice's grandfather on her mothers' side was called Jack. Like many others at the time he had emigrated from famine ravished Ireland to London to find a better life. He swapped rural outdoor farming work for a job at a cement factory somewhere outside London. Jack in his naivety, had imagined a wonderful life in London where money could be earned for those who worked hard. Jack was not looking for a glamourous or even successful life. He had compromised on those dreams many years ago watching his parents starve so that he and his brothers could eat.

Jack eventually met and married a local English woman who had also accepted life's disappointments. Having exchanged her dreams of becoming a nurse settled for the daily mundane chores of a housewife in suburban London. They had their first baby within a year of getting married. This was Alice's mother called Eileen.

Eileen grew up in a troubled house with her father Jack spending his hard-earned wages on alcohol and her mother grieving for a different life that she wished she had. Ultimately, Eileen formed the opinion that marriage was inevitably miserable. Some folks were destined to be unhappy with their lives she concluded. On leaving school, Eileen promptly moved away from her miserable parents and became a secretary for an insurance company in the Mid-West of England. Eileen got pregnant the following year after a short office romance. She moved back to grandparents in Ireland and Alice was born in catholic shame some nine months later.

Alice Kelly had decided in her early formative years that she would not accept the baton of failure passed down from her mother. She had ideas and plans and was determined that she would see them to fruition. Clever in junior and middle school, she excelled in mathematics and her mind was quick. She amazed even her teachers at how fast she should calculate algebra and other mathematical equations of a complexity that would not be out of place at a university institution.

After emigrating back to England to work as a school cleaner. Alice eventually won a scholarship at a University to study Computer Science. She applied herself with every fibre of her being. She took extra tuition; she almost lived in the tech lab and studied every book on computer science that she could get her hands on.

Eventually, graduating with a H1 in Computer Science she married the love of her life Frank Braithward and together they started a business in Information Technology with a particular expertise in designing electronic banking systems for large financial institutes.

The business had become successful before Frank had died of a heart attack that Alice always blamed on the stress of the business. The success of the business afforded them the trappings of wealth, but this was of limited consolation compared to the death of their daughter in her prime and before her time who left behind a young child. Their only grandchild.

The premature taking of her daughter had a great toll on Alice. She wished she could take the place of her deceased only daughter and decided that life was not fair. Maybe, that is just what life is supposed to be. Even life spent on the most worthwhile of pursuits, living the most intense of lives ultimately had no value. Perhaps it did not matter what you achieved or did with your life. Perhaps disappointment and failures mixed with splashes of achievement, wonder and beauty was the only expectation we should have for life itself. Perhaps, Alice thought, it was the expectation to achieve that made people disappointed and unhappy.

Some years later, Alice had invested the proceeds of her business and property portfolio into many charitable endeavours. She was a well-known Angel Investor in many start-ups including cancer and cognitive regeneration research companies. In fact, she maintained direct involvement in Neuroscience research and was one of the first to volunteer for trials in low frequency brain stimulation technology to prevent cognitive decline in healthy aging.

Now in her eighties, she demonstrated the cognitive acuity of someone half her age. She could process information and perform mental calculation with ease. Her Mini-Mental State Exam tests were off the chart and showed no signs of dementia. Her neuronal pathways continued to replenish, and normal age-related brain shrinkage was almost undetectable. Alice enjoyed her monthly mental acuity tests with her Doctor.

However, Alice's body was not on the same trajectory as her healthy brain organ and she experienced the natural progression of time on the rest of her body. Recently, she had undergone a double hip joint replacement that required a stay at a private care home for recuperation.

Alice did not mind staying at a care home facility. She saw it as a necessity to speed her body recovery. To some extent, she enjoyed the attention of the medical staff and was always eager to engage in discussions about all aspects of medical diagnosis.

On her admission to the Care Home, Alice was delighted to meet her Care Assistant and volunteer befriender. She looked forward to nice conversations over her favourite cup of tea.

Of course, the young Susan Birchfield, the volunteer care assistant who dabbled in Psychic manipulation of others, did not know anything about her new client.

SUSAN BIRCHFIELD

10 Weeks ago

Susan Birchfield was a self-professed psychic reader and a volunteer care giver and befriender of the elderly. And for a small fee, would profess to read your mind, tell your future, and offer advice on matters of the spirit. Of course, this was complete nonsense. Susan Birchfield was a confidence trickster. A bitter woman who was disappointed with her life and took some strange satisfaction from offering her own style of assistance to those less fortunate than herself. Unfortunately, Susan's client base was usually vulnerable residents in a Care Home where she worked as a volunteer.

Under the guise of a care giver volunteer, Susan had heard of a new intake of residents to the care home. One of the staff members at the centre had carelessly divulged over a tea break about a wealthy widower who was coming to stay with the home as part of a post-operative recovery plan. Her health condition determined that she would require 24 hr care and accordingly it was recommended by her personal physician Dr Ryan to place her in the care facility for three months. These guests always interested Susan. Firstly, they required others to take care of their needs. Secondly, they had a small family and thirdly, they had money.

Susan set about to research her new potential client. Alice Kelly was born in 1928 and married to Frank Braithward in 1948. Frank was a professional pilot and worked all his life in aviation. He had piloted during the second world war and was awarded the George Cross Medal for his efforts in 1944. Of interest to Susan, was that Frank had come from inherited money and his family were landlords for several significant value properties.

Alice's family originated from Ireland. They were from a farming background but google did not have too much information on her family. This did not put Susan off. Afterall, money is money she crudely thought.

Next steps were to research Alice's living relatives. She discovered that Alice and her husband Frank had a single child. A daughter Mary, who had died in the early eighties of pneumonia. Angela underlined this information in yellow highlighter deciding this could be especially important. The surviving grandson was David who was the only living relative for poor old Alice.

Susan decided that the next step would be to meet Alice in person. Susan already had access to the care centre through her 'volunteer' care provider capacity. This role was to visit elderly residents on a periodic basis to offer company through conversation. In Susan's mind, she was making a sacrifice of her time to talk to these lonely people at their time of need. In some cases, perhaps they had no one else or their family lived far away and could not visit so frequently.

There was also a home vicar and priest who held mass and visited with the patients. Susan did not like either of them. They were suspicious of Susan's motives and she found them both bothersome. Susan overheard from one of the receptionists that Father Brown had held prayers with Alice the previous week at her request. Angela concluded that Alice must be of the Catholic persuasion and this tied in with her Irish background. She decided that this would be the perfect introduction to her potential benefactor.

On the following week, after checking that the visitor record for Alice was empty, Susan decided to pay an introductory visit to Alice. As is normal during the day, the patient private room doors are always left open unless there is a nurse or doctor attending. Ensuring that her blue visitor pinafore was clean and ironed, and her name badge was prominent.

Susan liked that she had a uniform. It gave her a feeling of belonging and importance. Like a nurse but in a different way. Susan made a light tap on the open door and not waiting for an invite, walked into Alice's small care room.

'Hello, welcome to Golden Sun Care Home, how are you keeping? I'm Susan by the way'.

Alice looked up from her upright pillow position to see her unexpected visitor. She always liked to have a visitor and someone to talk to. She gladly welcomed her guest.

'I'm very well, thank you Susan. I'm Alice' she responded in a strong clear tone.

Susan was slightly surprised at this eighty something year old resident. Her alertness seemed good and she was able to pull herself up and adjust her back support without assistance. The first step is to establish a connection with the client that is warm, flattering and trusting. With a broad smile, Susan went straight to the bedside and placed her hand onto the arm of the old woman. Of course, Susan knew the effect of personal contact through touch and building connection. Alice responded positively to this contact and placed her right hand over the hand of Susan, so reinforcing the connection.

The appearance of a uniform gives the intended authoritative position. Susan continued her introduction patter as she had done so many times before. 'You are looking great' she continued deciding that this was now the time to give her new client a chance to speak.

'Thank you. Could you pass me a glass of water please if that's ok?'

'But of course,' responded Susan gently passing the small glass of water to the frail woman. 'And how is the family?' she continued.

Alice sips the water and hands it back to Susan who gladly accepts it placing it on the bedside counter just out of reach for Alice.

'Well, I only have a grandson left now and sure he has his own family now and can't visit as often.'

'Ah sure, that's the way of the world now isn't it' affirms Susan. But I am always available to visit you anytime you want to have a chat. In fact, I'm here tomorrow if you would like me to call into you again?' Not waiting for a response, Susan takes her leave committing to visit to her new client on the following day. Susan knows the importance of not overstaying her welcome on the first introduction meeting.

On the second day, Susan turns up at her afternoon visit time. She has decided to press on further with her new client. She knows not to get over specific. She must stay away from specifics at all cost and instead play a game of statistical norm. She knows full well that grief is a general emotion and is present in many situations.

'I had a strange dream last night Alice. I saw you as a young woman with a handsome man. You both looked so happy. But then I saw you upset, and I got a strong sense of grief. What do you think that means?'

Alice looks perplexed initially. But the visitor knows that clients will very often hear what they need to hear and disregard the rest. Under the right circumstances, susceptible people will believe what they want to believe and construct the words to fit their life circumstances. Most importantly, this reasoning occurs subconsciously and is processed by the brain in milliseconds. Susan waits for Alice to process the information and respond.

'That is amazing' speaks Alice. 'My late husband Frank was on my mind last night and I was thinking about his upcoming anniversary. But how did you know this?'

Susan is of course delighted with this response. Having tentatively established her astonishing gift, she uses the same strategy to deepen the connection. She wants her client to personalize wide ranging statements and make them apply to her alone. Moving closer to Alice, Susan touches her arm again and momentarily

71

closes her eyes for effect.

'I see an important person in your life' she says with a gentle smile.

Alice is now looking amazed. The wizen old woman acknowledges her grandson's existence and exclaims her wonder. 'Dear holy god, you are a gift that you can see inside me' she exclaims in her old Irish accent.

Susan decides that it is time to move on to the phishing stage. This stage is vital for Susan and constitutes approximately two thirds of psychic reading phenomena. It further builds the trust relationship necessary to extract financial reward for the effort.

'Losing your husband Frank when you did was difficult for you. But I can see that you are the sort of person who comes out of tragedies a little bit stronger and wiser'.

'It's true. It was difficult losing my Frank and then when my daughter died unexpectedly, I thought that I would never survive.'

'Bereavement is one of the hardest things that anyone can go through, but you should know that both are proud of you and wait for you on the other side.'

'Really?' asks Alice apparently unable to contain her amazement. 'I want to be here for them both and be strong until it is my time to join them.'

'I can organize an anniversary notice for the paper and mass dedication for them, if you'd like?' asks Susan. 'I don't think it is too expensive and you can sort the payment out with me afterwards.'

On leaving that day, Susan Birchfield concluded a very worthwhile visit and a new client with good potential that needed to be maximised for best return.

Alice on the other hand. Was slightly upset to talk of her deceased loved ones. But looked forward to the speaking with her new friend visitor again.

On the next visit from the volunteer care provider, Susan duly presented the receipts for the anniversary mass dedication and a contribution to lighting candles. Alice was a bit surprised at the amount but nonetheless reached for her purse and paid over the amount from her emergency monies. Susan took this opportunity to query how much cash Alice carried in her purse, adding that it was not safe to hold cash in the room.

'For security reasons, I can mind any cash for you in safe keeping.'

'It's only my weekly cash allowance that my grandson sends to me every Friday. I usually have it spent before the following Monday' explains Alice.

Susan was disappointed with this news. She realised to make this venture of interest she needed to raise the stakes. Small petty cash was not good enough.

Over the next few weeks, Susan made a visit twice a week to her new 'friend' delivering psychic readings that started to include predictions about financial burden. In turn, Alice appeared to become attached to her new companion and openly shared personal finance information. She told Susan that she had her late husband's inheritance still intact in an investment account earning good returns and was a shareholder in more than one company. This kept Susan's attention peaked.

The old woman appeared to relish the visits from her care giver and even encouraged her with her psychic reading. During one of the regular weekly visits, Alice asked Susan if she would go to the local bank for her to make a small withdrawal that required Alice to hand over her bank card and PIN number. Susan accepted readily.

Susan's suspicion about Alice's deposit balances was confirmed. Reading from the ATM balance screen, Susan was thrilled to note a 100K balance on account. 'After all these years of volunteer care service to these old rich people, I may just have found my golden goose'. She mused to herself.

With plan in play, Susan continued to visit Alice while at the same time researching conditions of withdrawal associated with Alice's deposit account. She had discovered through bank administration staff that large transactions were restricted and required a secondary signature in person at the bank. The best way to transfer funds from this deposit account was via electronic transfer that could be done remotely online. Susan was not exactly a computer expert but nonetheless concluded that this was the best direction forward to draw the least amount of attention to her. She figured, once I have the money, I can leave this job anyway and perhaps move to the coast. In Susan's mind at least, this sounded like a good plan.

The wily old Alice was so happy to have a new friend and she also felt that they knew each other well enough. Over the last week, she had a glowing glint in her eye and looked as sharp as a penny. She explained to Susan that she wanted to make a financial contribution to Alice directly to ease the financial burdens she had shared with her over the past weeks. This contribution was also to recognise her psychic skills and for helping her spend her petty cash weekly on stuff that she could not remember asking for. Alice said it was best that we do an electronic transfer from her bank account directly into Susan's account. We could do it from the bed using a tablet device that Alice had received from her grandson. All that was needed was the IBAN for Susan's bank account and passcodes so that the transfer can be made.

Susan was of course overjoyed. She had worked for many years slaving for others. Sure, she had a small stash of 20,000 euro accumulated from her psychic reading trickery, but she saw this as just a drop in the ocean compared to what she planned to take from this old biddy. Her mind was filled with holiday plans, shopping sprees, maybe a car. She complimented herself on how clever she was and that she deserved everything coming to her.

The following morning, Susan was early for her visit to her old friend, soon to be benefactor. She kissed her on the cheek and told Alice how fantastic she looked for a woman of her age. Alice of course took the compliments without gushing. However, she looked different this morning. She was certainly not as frail looking and had all her smarts about her.

'Ah yes, good to see you again my friend' spoke Alice as she plumped her own pillows to sit upright.

'You are looking fresh this morning' beamed Susan in anticipation of her gain.

Alice pulled out a tablet iPad from under the sheets that Susan had not seen before.

'Where did you get that from?' asked Susan.

'Oh, it's just a toy my grandson sent into me. He said it would help me stay connected to the world. 64gb, built in SIM. It is a super-fast data processing device.

Susan was not too computer savvy but had seen these tablet devices before. Although she was surprised that Alice was clearly familiar with the operation of it. She looked on as Alice logged-in and connected to an online banking portal screen.

'How much do you want from me?' asked Alice still focused on the tablet screen.

Susan was surprised at the directness of the question.

'I just couldn't. I mean, I have financial problems that are wearing me down, but perhaps I could take a loan that would help me out. You are so kind and generous my friend. But if you could see your way to loaning me 50,000 euro this would be a great help to me.'

Alice looked up from the small screen for a second and stared towards the upper corner of her room as though making a calculation in her mind. She turned back to the screen and moved her fingers across the keypad entering information.

'Now Susan. I will need your account number, sort code, name, and address of your bank so I can make the transfer. Please enter the details and follow the instructions from the screen.'

Susan did not hesitate. Her mind filled with greed and her own sense of entitlement. She duly took the tablet device in her hand and typed the numbers from her account card into the screen. Once entered, the device prompted the user to return to receiver account holder. She handed the device back to Alice to complete the transaction as requested.

Alice accepted it back and completed out the online form. With a final scan of the details, she held her index finger in mid-air for a moment. Then, as though pressing a doorbell, she landed her index finger to the touch screen.

'Now, that's done' she exclaimed finally.

Susan was finding it difficult to contain her excitement and in her mind was already seeing her new bank balance.

'Thank you, Alice. You are indeed a true friend' she mustered as she gathered herself to leave as quickly as possible. 'I will get it back to you as soon as possible!'

'Are you staying for some breakfast tea?' asked Alice as she put away the tablet device.

'Unfortunately, I don't have the time' she blurted out. Her care pretence starting to fade. 'I need to be somewhere else right now.' This was her final words as she turned to walk out the door.

'I doubt you'll go far' responded Alice from her bed that stopped Susan in her tracks for a moment as she looked back at the smiling old woman.

Susan Birchfield shook her head and did all she could not to break into a run down the corridor. She stopped momentarily at her supervisor's office and threw her volunteer access card on to her desk followed by choice words about never stepping foot back in this place. Susan almost danced her way out the front doors of the Care Home that morning for the very last time she thought.

It is true though, under the correct circumstances, people hear and see what they need to.

Susan made her way home through the traffic she was slightly annoyed that her old car was running out of fuel and needed to stop at the next filling station. As she tanked up, she felt as though she had won the lottery and found it difficult to contain her excitement. I am so smart she told herself as she stood in the queue to pay.

'Pump number five please' as she passed her debit card to the teller.

The first indication of a problem was the beeping tone and red light from the card reader.

'I'm sorry, but your card is declined. Do you perhaps have another one?'

Susan leaned towards the Perspex divider and shouted back through the hole.

'Impossible. Try it again.'

This time however, the gas station attendant shook his head and passed Susan's card back to her through the small gap in the security screen. 'Your card is declined.'

Susan quickly rummaged through her small purse and routed out what was left of Alice's weekly allowance from her grandson. She just about had enough to cover the fuel and indignantly shoved the collection of coins and notes through the teller's payment hatch.

She barged her way out of the gas station and made her way to the nearest ATM machine as quickly as she could. Placing the card in the machine she entered her six-digit pin code as she had done earlier on Alice's iPad.

BALANCE AVAILABLE = 00,00.00 FUNDS TRANSFER COMPLETE

DREAMS

Susan Birchfield always had a problem accepting herself, who she was and who she had become. From as far back as she could remember, she had developed a complex of never good enough. She was brought up in a single parent family and had never known her father. Her mother had her own insecurities that had influenced the behavioural pattern of Susan as a young child. She was taught from an early age that the welfare system was an entitlement to be used and abused to get as much as possible from state support. Her mother practiced this belief with great effect until prescription drug abuse and alcohol dependency limited her capacity to care for anyone. Gradually, and without consideration, Susan assumed the role of care giver for her mother from an early age foregoing her education and teenage friendship development.

She could only imagine what it was like to accept herself completely. Every mistake through her young life made a mark on Susan just as deep as every self-inflicted cut on her body. She could recall every dream that had vanished and every pain that she had felt over her thirty years life span.

Susan Birchfield woke that morning with a half empty bottle of vodka still in her hand. A plastic cup on the floor beside the armchair she had woken in. Her eyes focused. Her small single bedroom flat was dark and musty. The dampness was coming through the walls causing the wallpaper above the old blocked up fireplace to peel as though teasing the occupant who lived in this grovel. The events of the last week swirled in Susan's head. Her thoughts taunted her by reminding her she had lost all her money to a patient in a care home. She vowed to get revenge on the old woman. She would get her money back and more or disappear forever, never coming back to this place.

After sobering up and eating a breakfast of stale cornflakes, Susan still had no plan. She had thrown the access card back to her supervisor and told her to stick the job. In hindsight, this might have been hasty she thought. She had called her bank who had confirmed what she already knew and told her that her accounts were empty. Susan realised how stupid she had been. How could I have fallen for that trick she thought to herself?

Susan knew which room Alice occupied in the Care Home and although she could not get into the building, she decided to make her way to the window that she could look in at Alice and let her know she was coming. Perhaps she could scare Alice into refunding her.

Alice on the other hand was in particularly good form. Her recovery was proceeding well, and she was considering leaving the care home at the end of this week. The Care Staff had told her that there was no reason that she would not be back on her feet in the coming weeks and that a full recovery was expected. In the last week, she noticed that she was experiencing vivid dreams and although this did not bother her too much, she would wake confused and disorientated that lasted a few minutes. She had also asked her nurse to close the window blinds as once or twice she thought she saw someone from outside looking in through the window.

Susan sat on the wall across from the building watching the Care Home. Fuming. Angry. Biting her lower lip. She wanted to rush in and kill that old woman. She spent most of the day watching the comings and goings from the Care Home before finally giving up and walking home.

Later, as darkness started to fall, Susan arrived back to her small flat despondent with life. She ate some stale food from her fridge not even sure what it was. She found a bottle of sleeping tablets and briefly considered taking the whole bottle before finally dispensing out two and knocking them back quickly followed by a glass of vodka. She slumped down into the alcohol stained chair and quickly fell into a deep sleep.

Back at the care home, Alice had a visit from her neuro cognitive science specialist who wanted to check up on her progress. He was standing in for Doctor Ryan while he was on his vacation somewhere in Mexico she remembered.

Alice told him about her vivid dreams of late and wondered if this could be a side effect from the high dose of synthetic tyrosine she was taking as part of the study trial to improve neuroplasticity in healthy aging. Wired up to a portable modified EEG, her brain scans showed high levels of activity in her medial temporal lobes and memory centres. This is not particularly unusual in healthy brains, but activity was higher than expected when taking in Alice's age profile.

That night, Alice also fell into a deep sleep and entered REM state. Behind her closed eye lids, her eyeballs danced and moved from side to side with no rhythm or predictability. In this dream state, she saw her adversary and ex care assistant, Susan Birchfield driving in her car. Alice watched from a position in the back seat as the car hurtled at speed down an unrecognised road in the dark. On-coming headlights flashed to signal danger to the driver, but the driver did not react. Both hands on the steering wheel showed the whites of Susan's knuckles as she held firm to her direction. The noise of the highly revved engine in the small car was almost deafening. From the back seat, Alice looked up and glimpsed Susan's blood shot eyes staring back at her from the rear-view mirror. She felt the rage and anger in those eyes.

Alice was startled awake and blinked her eyes in quick succession to regain her bearings and focus. She could hear her monitors beeping a high heart rate and turned to scan her small room. After a minute regaining her reality, she sat up in the bed and stared down at her feet poking out from under her covers. She shook herself and realised that she had dreamed. However, she could still feel the desperation of her ex care worker to whom she had taught a brutal lesson. Alice tossed and turned that night. She could not get the image of those eyes from her thoughts and knew inside that this game was not yet over and determined that she must make the next move.

TIME SHIFT

Time Shift INC is a research neuroscience clinic established through a small group of angel investors that included Alice and Frank Braithward. Time Shift Inc owned diverse interests in businesses that included shareholdings in Care Homes, Private Psychiatric Care and a shelf company called The Disappearing Shop. The company directors rationalised this diverse business model as necessary to support its primary research goals and to provide a suitable and accessible participant pool through these diverse company assets.

Although her husband Frank had died some years ago of a heart attack, Alice who was in her eighties, kept her hand in the business and attended regularly at board meetings. Over time, she had steadily increased her stock holding and accordingly had significant influence on the company's research direction.

The primary research focus of the company was brain wave entrainment to treat cognitive decline and disease in healthy aging. To-date, the institute had some modest success in alleviating symptoms of migraine and uncontrolled limb tremor through applications of resonance entrainment of low frequency signals in the Alpha frequency range. Indeed, Alice herself was always the first to sign up for participant trials and always pushed the research associates for faster and broader reach research directions.

This created some tension among the research associates who felt that Alice was pushing the institute outside of ethical boundaries for research. Alice believed that aging is a biological process that resulted from the functional decline in neurotransmitter metabolism. Ultimately, this resulted in a slowing in alpha frequency brainwaves that were detectable and read from an EEG scan. Alice Braithward, through her research company Time Shift Inc, sought to find ways to prevent, or slow, cognitive decline through brainwave entrainment interventions. Of particular interest to Alice, was deep brain stimulation and thought transfer. She wanted to be able to transfer her thoughts to another person by manipulating brainwave signals. Ultimately, to experience life through her mind in a younger and more able body.

However, Alice herself was becoming living proof of the institute's potential. Her cognitive ability was extraordinary for her age. She was frequently tested using the standard dementia questionnaires and each time passed with flying colours. She had the brain function of a person half her age with no signs of cognitive decline. Her memory retention was excellent, and she could recite back a 7-digit number recall with ease. However, Alice was never satisfied. She would embark on her own 'research' and would speak to any 'expert' regardless of claim validity. More recently, she was investigating synthetic versions of neurotransmitters, naturally created chemicals essential for brain high level processing and communication. She combined these chemical neurotransmitters with low frequency brainwave entrainment technology to create a resonate frequency brainwave pattern.

It was long suspected that Alice was taking much higher dosages than recorded in the clinical trial protocols. Many of the research associates were worried that Alice was taking the concept too far but felt they could not express concerns openly due to the financial influence that Alice held over the company.

Under the financial influence of Alice Braithward, and in contravention of ethical standards, Time Shift INC had started trials in evaluating dream state transference from one participant to another. This involved the inducing of deep sleep dream conditions from a control subject and transferring the dream experience to a target host. Essentially, Alice wanted to experience the dreams of others. To become a part of someone else's dreams. To experience the emotions and thoughts of another person through a dream state and ultimately influence their thought patterns.

Alice believed that her recent vivid dream episodes were related to her secret self-dosing of brain chemicals with synthetic alternatives. Susan Birchfield had accidently, become an unwilling participant in Alice's private trials.

That morning, Alice picked up the newspaper and read the news of the mysterious disappearance of a local befriender volunteer and Care Home Worker, Susan Birchfield. The article went on to describe how caring Susan was, and that all her friends and associates were shocked and worried about her missing. Alice recalled her lucid dreams from a previous night and wondered if Susan had perhaps crashed her car. But that did not make sense, surely the wreck of her car would be found and reported immediately. The article contained a nice picture of Susan. She looked much younger and nicer in the picture. Much different than Alice had experienced from this woman in person.

Later that evening, Alice heard on the news that Susan's body had been found in a river some miles downstream from the town. However, Alice was not really surprised to read that she had drowned.

The Consultant had finally given Alice and her care team clearance to be released. She was happy to be getting out of the care home. Her recuperation following the hip replacement operation was over and she felt well enough to walk aided by a stick. She committed to herself that after two weeks more the stick would not be required. Alice placed a call to her driver and told him to collect her from the Care Home within the hour. She was not going to stay a minute longer in this care home and anxious to get back to her work, she had already notified the test clinic that she was to attend for brain sequencing trials later that afternoon.

On time, exactly one hour later, Alice's driver appeared at her room door. After a gentle knock on the open door to signal his presence, Alice beckoned the man to enter.

'Good. Can you please collect my bags Jeffery and place them in the car? Then come back inside for me as I'd like your arm to escort me to the car.'

'Yes of course Mam' acknowledged the tall uniformed driver.

Some minutes later and Alice was departing the Care Home through the main doors to the waiting car. The Driver held the back door and taking her walking cane, guided her into the back seat of the polished car.

DETERMINATION

8 Weeks ago.

The local authorities' investigation into the disappearance of Susan Birchfield had determined the cause of death to be drowning. The family was particularly aggrieved by this finding. They had argued now for months that the reported head trauma injuries should be considered as suspicious and that her behaviour on the days leading up to her disappearance was highly out of character. However, the medical examiner concluded that the head injuries most likely occurred from falling from the bridge and head impact against rocks as the body was carried downstream.

Susan's car had been found abandoned a couple of days after she was discovered. It was clean inside and not just tidy. I mean it was spotless inside, no rubbish, papers and the dashboard plastic had been polished. None of those paper parking receipts, not a pen or a sticky note, not a crumb. Susan's family pointed to this as usual stating that Susan was not a tidy person. They argued that Susan had never cleaned the car.

The family also pointed to her unusual behavioural markers the days and weeks before her disappearance. In particular, she had walked out of her volunteer job as a befriender at the Care Home without an explanation. This made no sense to her family and few friends. Testimony from family said that she loved caring for the old and infirm and gave her time willingly to help where she could. Her few friends were less vocal, and their opinions did not get published in the local media. Her employers at the Care Home also had no comment. Eventually, the Justice for Susan movement grew quiet as the winter came in and they eventually disappeared or moved on to the next Justice for someone campaign.

The management committee at The Disappearing Shop met every quarter to go through the cases of the last three months. This was a sort of lessons learned exercise, where under the culture of continuous improvement, the business looked to improve on its practice and procedures. The format of the lessons learned was always the same. The board and associates went through a performance appraisal for each case and a final rating determined based on key performance metrics. These performance metrics included measurable attributes such as schedule, cost, and quality of service.

The disappearance of Susan Birchfield as a care assistant from Felixstowe was discussed. In terms of pre-planning, schedule, plan adherence and execution. There was a discussion regarding the pre-planning stage and perhaps a tardiness in the personality profiling. It was felt collectively that a more in-depth profile should have been developed for this client. Afterall, the basis of the engagement was that Susan was a failed business owner with financial difficulties. And while this was true to some extent, the profile report did not identify that she was a care worker, and her business interest was ripping off elderly care residents.

'And how would this additional information have made a difference?' asked one of the associates.

'A medical professional could have drawn a lot of attention.'

'She was not a medical professional. She was a visitor to homes of the elderly.'

The debate went on around the table amongst the suited members of the panel.

'Ok. I think we have debated this point long enough' spoke the Chairperson. 'Let us move on to the execution phase. How does the group feel the plan was executed?'

'I thought it went very well' spoke the Project Manager, Philip Burns.

'There was some initial resistance at the final moments, but these were dealt with quickly and effectively.'

'Do you mean that you bludgeoned her to death with a brick? 'asked one of the associates.

'I did what needed to be done in that moment' was the cold response.

Each around the table cast their eyes down to avoid eye contact with the PM who searched around the table for anyone to catch his eye. All except for one person.

'I think you made a pigs ear of a simple job. It was a third rate mess'.

The Project Manager was not happy about this public rebuke.

'Really, that's a surprise. And what do you consider to be the mess exactly?'

'Do you think it was necessary to club the woman to death like you did?'

The Project Manager was now irritated and struggled to contain himself and maintain his professional exterior persona. He picked up his white plastic cup and sipped on his water as a calming exercise. Shrugging his shoulders and fixing his tie, the PM looked agitated.

'Ok, let us all just calm things down a bit. There should be no personal recriminations at these review sessions. We are here to learn from past jobs and do things better in the future'; interjected the Chairperson.

'But this client was recommended by yourself madam chair. And, if I recall correctly, with some insistence on the urgency.' The Project Manager was now using his hands to convey his point and looked around the table at his associates for support.

The Chairperson glared back at this young Project Manager. She knew this PM quiet well and was initially surprised by his defensive response. Philip was a rough diamond. He was street savvy and knew how to take care of himself. She had hired Philip many years ago. Gave him a chance to change his life circumstance. To walk away from street violence and make something of himself.

She leaned forward onto her elbows and surveyed the team around the table. They read from her body language not to intervene and to wait.

'As a general rule, high levels of anxiety are detrimental to individual performance. I can accept that you had an anxious moment on the bridge. However, that does not excuse your actions. You acted in anger. Like an animal. In that moment you lost control and beat a woman to death with a brick that was not part of the plan.'

Philip kept his eyes down during this redress from his superior.

'But Mrs Braithward, the client became argumentative that morning on the bridge. The situation became unpredictable and I responded in the moment and did what I had to do. For you! For this organization!'

Alice Braithward looked at the young man half her age. Then surveyed the rest of the committee seated at the table. Stone faced, grey expressionless men.

'Yes Philip. And I must now make a decision in the best interest of this organization.'

That said, Alice lifted her eyes and another grey suit stepped forward and placed a clear plastic bag over Philip's head holding it tight as he struggled. His legs kicked out under the table as though a frog on its back trying desperately to correct its position. However, his eyes rolled momentarily, and he finally gave up the struggle resigned to his fate.

'Next time. Follow the fucking plan' she says turning back to the agenda.

DREAM TRAVEL

Alice felt comfortable as she lay back on the bed. She felt someone reach in across her face and adjust her covers. She opened her eyes momentarily and looked at the clinic ceiling. Her periphery vison picked up movement of the white lab tech coats as they busied themselves with preparations. Alice adjusted the large headphones on her ears. Sometimes they felt heavy she thought and started to slip if she moved in the bed. She could also feel the multi-probes attached to her head. The wires feeding back to a colour monitor that annoyingly bleeped every now and then. As Alice blinked, someone leaned across into her vision. 'Are you ready to commence Alice?'

Alice nodded her head without speaking. She was just eager to get started and thinning her patience with the bustle around her while she lay flat on her back looking at the ceiling. Someone made a final adjustment of the headphones covering Alice's ears that signalled ready to commence. Alice closed her eyes and breathed deeply. The white noise sound through the headphones masked a low frequency signal intended to stimulate the olivary cortex deep in the brain and generate a resonate frequency in the delta range. At this frequency, the brain is below conscious thought and in a deep regenerative sleep state.

Finally, she felt the warmth of an infusion through her left arm. Alice felt her consciousness shut down as she drifted away. What seemed like no time, Alice was standing outdoors looking across at the main entrance of a shopping centre mall. She scanned around her as she absorbed her new surroundings. It was a bright day, and she felt a cold breeze bristle the hair on her arms.

She glanced down at the feet and legs of a young woman in flats and a swing dress. A woollen jumper over a baggy t-shirt. Alice did not recognise the host.

In her left hand, Alice noticed that she was holding a red string that trailed off into the distance. Her instinct was to follow the string that led towards the main shopping centre entrance. The string was loosely laying along the ground almost like an electrical cable and it went through her fingers easily as she followed its path into the shopping mall. Alice noticed that all the individual shop units were closed. The entire shopping mall was closed, and she was the only person in there. The red string trailed off into the distance around the advertisement billboards and Alice followed. As she came to the first corner, she noticed in the distance a small group standing together in a circle. The red string led directly to them. Alice approached wondering who this group could be. The string came up off the shopping mall floor and disappeared into the pocket of one of the men talking in the group. Alice was not sure if she should disturb the conversation, and they continued as though she was not there.

'Excuse me' asked Alice in a soft tone not recognising her own voice.

The man in the brown suit did a double take mid-sentence and looked at Alice.

Alice recoiled as she recognised the youthful face of her deceased husband Frank Braithward. He was much younger, perhaps mid-twenties but his features still instantly recognizable to her.

'Can I help you?' he asked in a direct tone and not recognizing Alice.

'Erm… is your name Frank?'

'Yes, are you lost child?'

These were the last sounds that Alice heard as she felt a jolt to her brain and was instantly transported out of the scene. As desperate as she was to stay in that moment, she knew that it was gone.

The lights that Alice had experienced before, fuzzed and flashed inside her mind's eye. They looked like multi coloured flashlights of people lost on a dark hillside shining their beams for direction. Alice could now hear voices. They were not speaking to her but instead a collection of voices talking over each other at the same time. A murmuring of sounds that got louder and louder.

As Alice's eyes came into focus, she saw a woman standing on a cliff side with an old man in a wheelchair. Alice could feel the raw emotions of hurt and desperation course through her. The old man looked out to sea from his wheelchair and looked content. She sensed his emotions of regret and sorrow. As much as she tried not to, Alice felt drawn into the emotions of the young woman holding her father's wheelchair. A sound of a cell phone rang urgently. Alice looked to her left hand and lifted it to her ear. As she did so, the wheelchair released and disappeared over the cliff edge.

Alice's brain swirled as visions of events flashed before her like a giant carousel of images. The scenes moved fast and appeared as a coloured blur and then slowed so that it looked as though changing channels on a giant television screen. Alice looked intensely at the images as they swirled past her. She lifted a hand and placed her index finger into the moving images as they slowed and eventually stopped before her. She looked on at a scene of woman standing on a bridge as it played out before her. She appeared to be having an argument with someone else just out of view. Her arms waved angrily as she tried to express her opinions. A few times she slapped her hands against her sides as though frustrated with the situation or what the other person was saying or not saying. Alice was frustrated that she could not hear the conversation on the bridge. She leaned closer and turned her head as though trying to tune her hearing. Alice could only hear muffled sounds from the arguing pair. She watched as the argument developed. Suddenly, the man stepped forward and struck the woman with a red brick across the side of her head. She slumped heavily to the ground and Alice watched in horror as he repeatedly struck the woman on the ground. She had long since stopped moving when the beating eventually stopped.

Alice felt her consciousness return. It felt as though waking from a deep sleep. Her mind buzzed from her dreams and thoughts as she slowly became aware of the room she was in. Someone lifted the headphone set from her ears and Alice's hearing started to come back to the people around her. She could hear the monitors beep every now and then as though to remind them she had a heartbeat. Alice blinked her eyes open to the room. Her thoughts still raced at the scenes as she recalled moments of her dreams. She felt confused as her conscious mind ran through the process of determining what is real and its priority rating and then expeditiously assigning everything else as imagination or dreams to be fragmented and stored in short term memory only.

Post-Trial Review

Alice was disappointed at this latest trial and her experience. She looked around at the white coat clinicians and researchers that surrounded the small table waiting for her to reveal her experiences. She felt her fingers tingle as though pins and needles in her fingertips. She decided this was not worth mentioning at this point.

'I experienced lucid dreaming, but they were highly fragmented. My dreams jumped from one experience to another, but I could not interact with or influence the dream characters.'

Each of the white coats scribbled notes as Alice spoke while scratching their chins.

'At 3.8Hz we noticed high levels of brain activity in the long-term memory centres. Did your dreams include past events from your history perhaps?

'Yes. I saw my husband as a young man. But it was fleeting, and he appeared to not recognize me as though perhaps I was someone else.'

Again, the note taking.

'I also saw events that I did not recognise. Nor did I recognise any of the participants. I felt as if I was watching someone else's life unravel.'

More note taking. Alice waited for a question or a response.

'And how are you feeling now?' came the Doctors question finally.

'I feel fine' lied Alice.

Her head throbbed and she experienced what she called lightning shots in her brain.

A nurse entered the room and placed blood work results and EEG scan prints onto the desk. Each of the gathered clinicians gathered up a page each and began scanning the printed information while using their pen as a pointer.

'Well, everything seems fine on our side' spoke the Doctor to nods from his colleagues. 'I think we should be ready to commence a heightened test tomorrow morning Alice if that suits you?'

Alice was already on her feet. 'Yes of course. Thank you Doctors.'

LIGHTS IN OUR EYES

3 Weeks ago.

Given the opportunity, most of us are generally more than happy to seek revenge and to right a wrong done against us. Revenge is one of the deepest instincts we have and an evolved trait of human nature. Across history, endless lives have been destroyed in an effort to settle scores even when there is no apparent benefit from taking a revenge action.

After taking her daily dose of synthetic neuro stimulators, Alice carefully placed the headphones over her ears and lay back willing sleep to take her to a dream state. The multiple frequency brain probes attached to her head made her look like someone from a science fiction movie. The combination of technology combined with the aged appearance of Alice contrasted sharply. An old woman connected to new equipment in a desperate attempt to challenge nature. She waited silently for the cocktail of synthetic brain stimulants to take effect.

Outside Alice's brain, the EEG monitors clicked and displayed brain frequency as though monitoring lightning storm activity moving across a vast plain. Alice's brain fired across both hemispheres signalling multiple brain centre activity as she slipped into a dream state. The neuronal networks fired, disabling old redundant pathways, and creating new ones as though a master builder at work on a grand scheme invisible to those outside. The monitors displayed frequency spikes and final quieting of activity as Alice's brain frequency fluctuation decreased and reached a condition not unlike transcendental meditative conditions. Looking down on Alice, she looked frail. Like a sleeping child in some ways. Vulnerable and dependant.

Inside Alice's brain, the superior olivary nuclei deep in the brain fired and transmitted multiple low frequency signals that create a resonance effect within the brain organ. In turn, the brain isolates part of the nervous system to disable reflex movements in limbs and other non-essential sensory capabilities. Heart and breathing rates are reduced. Within this biological masterpiece, Alice's brain creates a world that the unconscious manipulates and presents to the host. It is imagination presented in a way that appears and feels real.

Like an old movie reel, images flash before her eyes. At first, the images are black and white out of focus. It is hard to make out what they are as they blend into each other. Slowly, as the reel turns, colour appears, and the images start to slow and become more focused. Alice can also sense. Her emotions, her feelings, her senses are active that combine to induce a new reality contained in her subconscious state. Sounds are heard. At first in the distance but then drawing closer.

Alice slowly becomes aware of her new surroundings. She is standing outside in a cloudless sky, bright sunlight with a light summer breeze. Looking down, she is barefoot wearing a white petticoat smock to her knees. The sun feels warm and comforting on her skin. A lone tree close by is rustling from the breeze through its leaves and she is surrounded by tall grass moving back and forwards like an ocean of green and gold. Alice's emotions are that of joy and happiness. She stretches out her arms behind her and looks up towards the blue sky feeling the youthfulness of her body as she inhales deeply. A sound in the distance calls her attention as the image reel begins to change. Alice looks to the direction of the sound and strains her hearing to try to make it out. Slowly, the image setting changes and Alice feels an uncomfortable sensation on her inner ears. Coming into focus, Alice realises that she is in the cockpit of an aeroplane. Her seatbelt is uncomfortably tight, and she feels the vibration of the aircraft as it adjusts its position through hydraulic moving parts. A uniformed young man shouts into her face an instruction that she momentarily does not understand.

'Push down now!'

Alice looks down at the levers and gauges before her and almost instinctively her hands grab hold of the control columns. She turns one direction, then the other. She flicks a switch that activates hydraulics within the craft.

'Landing gear down and locked' she shouts over the noise.

In the moments that follow, Alice's heartrate and breathing increase on the monitors. She presses hard on the pedals at her feet. The sound is the screeching of metal and rubber components in contact as the brakes apply combined with the roar of reverse thrust on the engines.

Here, at this point, Alice's mind perception changes yet again. She finds herself among the last of the passengers preparing to disembark from the aircraft. As she nears the exit door, she notices a young man in pilots uniform looking at her from the other side of the queue. The confused look on his face is momentary. He nods an acknowledgment and gentlemanly signals to let Alice exit the door before him.

MIND SHOCKS

2 Weeks ago.

Alice felt a sharp shock to her brain as though someone had just stuck an electric cattle prod into her head. The sensation was like electricity – it pulsed her brain that caused an involuntary jerk of her left arm. She thought she could feel the pulse travel from her brain to the back of her ear, down her neck, to her shoulder and down her arm. But it was quick. It lasted less than a second and was always followed by a jerk reaction of her arm and a high-pitched ringing sound in her ear. Yes, it frightened Alice but the effect seemed to be short lived and within minutes the ringing sound stopped, and everything seemed normal. Or as normal as before the event.

However, the incident frequency rate appeared to be increasing. Instead of rarely occurring, it seemed to happen now as routine occurring approximately an hour after waking from lucid dreaming. Alice had decided not to tell the program research assistants for fear that they might discover that she was taking more of the synthetic supplements than recorded in the trial protocol. Alice rationalised this action by concluding that the research assistants were too conservative and did not understand the wider benefits of what she wanted to achieve. She still hoped, no, correction, she was determined to defy the biological certainty of aging and find a new host for her wonderful mind.

She wanted to cast aside the limitations of her aging and failing body. She had long ago determined that we are the essence of our minds and that our brain has the capacity to live beyond the life span of the weaker body. Through brain resonance, to predetermined natural low frequencies, she had managed to prevent cognitive decline that was previously thought to be inevitable only ten years previously. Her brain neuroplasticity had surged, and she felt as sharp in her mind as she did fifty years ago. The lucid dreaming, she believed, was her entry path to a new, younger, more vitalised body where her mind could live on in her new host body. A few mind shocks here and there for a milli-second seemed a worthwhile side effect she thought.

Philip Burns was an angry and violent young man. He had grown up experiencing violence throughout his entire formative years. He stepped in to take the punches for his mother and then later for his younger siblings on many occasions. Each time it became easier.

As Philip grew up, he moved between victim and survivor mentality readily depending on the moment or the situational context. In victim mode, he got sympathy from Social Workers and sometimes even the Police. Philip felt justified in victim mode. It excused his failings and Philip had many.

In survivor mode, he was aggressively defensive and over-reacted to criticism or well-intended advice. Initially, he drifted in and out of these two conditions as he wanted. However, as time progressed, it became a behavioural pattern that was more in control of him. Philip was reactive and under certain circumstance lost control and erupted into an uncontrollable rage. It was so intense, that he would have little recollection of the event. Essentially, his fight for survival responses took control of his brain and rational thought, his executive function, was temporarily disabled. This reduced Philip to a primitive raging animal.

Alice Braithward had come across this young man when he worked as a temporary driver for her. She had recognised the natural intelligence about him combined with the rawness of his emotions that carried forward from his early youth. She encouraged him to read. She listened to his opinions and a strange or unusual mutual recognition developed between them. He was awestruck by her wealth, her power and intelligence. She, by his youthfulness, animalistic aura, and potential.

Sometime later, Alice had offered Philip a small office job with development opportunities to a Project Manager with one of her companies. Initially, Philip was suspicious of the offer and his victim mentality background told him that he did not deserve an opportunity. However, Alice was persistent and patient and eventually coaxed her new interest into accepting the role on a trial basis. Alice was intrigued with Philip. She saw his raw emotions and a lack of self-control as a challenge to be overcome by a smarter mind. Just like hers.

Just after midnight, Alice laid her weary body down on the fresh clean linen sheets she could so easily afford. She reflected on the unfairness of a degenerating body while her mind was rewiring and renewing itself. To some extent, she blamed science. Here she was, doing her part to extend human life span by preventing or at least deferring cognitive decline in aging. After all, Bowhead Whales are mammals just like humans, and they can live beyond 200 years with no signs of age-related impairments that seems to afflict the human brain. Alice liked this comparison between humans and whales and saw no reason why humans should have an average life span of 85 years.

'And I should be content to live only to that age?' she said to herself out loud.

'I don't think so' was the answer back from her brain.

Later that night Alice had drifted off to sleep to rest her weary body and her mind let itself out to wander its dream world as though on an exercise routine.

Her mind visited different scenes and flicked through them with ease. It was like watching a subscription television channel and flicking through the hundreds of channels at random. Sometimes, Alice's mind would linger in the host's dream world. Watching. Listening. Experiencing the emotions of the episode. She watched as a man who was knocked off his bike and she viewed his mind, his thoughts, as he lay unconscious on the roadway. She watched as a young wife plotted to kill her husband by throwing him overboard on a cruise. She also saw people who she did not know that had lost their minds and become so blank inside. It was as if the blackboard of their thoughts, their mental being, had been wiped clean and she was the chalk waiting for instruction or direction. Each episode seemed to strengthen Alice's resolve to connect with these other minds in some way.

At approximately 4 am, Alice felt a mind shock hit her hard and she was jolted awake. Her left arm jumped involuntarily as though a reflex reaction and she felt the return signal run from her wrist, to her arm, to her neck, to just behind her ear and back into her brain stem. It felt like a low frequency electrical pulse sent out by the brain and returned through the nervous system of her left arm. She made a fist on her left hand, holding it for a couple of seconds before repeating like a squeeze action. She looked down at her wrist and watched the sinews in her wrist twitch with each squeeze before finally stretching the arm.

The uncomfortable awakening ensured that Alice would not sleep for the rest of the morning. She decided that her mind transfer program needed to move on to the next stage.

CLASS & STYLE

'Hello Kimberly, how nice to see you' spoke Alice in a soft tone becoming of her age. The Doctor's wife, or to be precise, his widow, turned on her high heels to look down on the old woman. Her manufactured fingernails resembled the claws of a bird of prey as they deftly wrapped around the wine glass.

Kimberly Ryan was defined in some circles as a classy bird. She was tall, slim, leggy and wore a dress that looked like she was poured into it. Her favourite expression was 'really'. She said this a lot, with a slight American accent that sounded fake or perhaps she had heard it on a reality television program.

'Do I know you?'

'You won't remember me, but I was an acquaintance of your husband Doctor Ryan before his unfortunate accident. I wanted to express my sympathy to you on his passing.'

Kimberly Ryan made a strange expression and briefly looked to the floor before lifting her beautiful eyes back to Alice. And those eyes. They were stunning.

'Really? I am sorry, your right I do not remember you. But thank you, I appreciate your thoughts.'

Kimberly turned on her nimble perfectly formed legs like a model making the turn at the end of a catwalk. Her gorgeous blonde hair followed.

Alice could not help looking this woman up and down. It was a strange sensation, but somehow, she felt oddly physically attracted to her. I could do some damage there she said crudely. Don't be so silly, what is wrong with you Alice, your eighty years old, get a grip woman! She told herself.

'Excuse me Kimberly' Alice called after the woman. A bit louder this time. With more intent or focus.

Kimberly was mid-sentence with someone else when she did a double take and looked back at Alice. She excused herself from the gentleman she was talking to and walked purposely back to stand a bit closer to Alice.

Alice inhaled Kimberly's expensive but subtle perfume. It suited her she thought.

'Are you Ok, did you want to say something else to me?' asked Kimberly.

'Erm..., I wondered if we might have a small chat about a delicate matter concerning your late husband.'

Kimberly was curious now.

This time she looked the old woman up and down. It did not take long as there was not too much of her to look at. Kimberly wondered was she a distant relation of David's, that she had forgotten. Not that it mattered much to the fish eating whatever is left of him she thought.

'You see, I knew your late husband in a professional capacity. He told me you had booked a cruise holiday and I just wondered what happened that he ended up lost overboard?'

Kimberly stared at the old woman before her.

'Really' she said moving her face closer to Alice. 'Perhaps we should take a seat.'

Alice was not great on her legs and was happy to take a seat. Her hip pain was starting to flare up again, probably something to do with the weather or perhaps standing for too long. The fragility of her body annoyed her.

'Yes, I was incredibly surprised to hear of your husband's unfortunate accident during your cruise holiday. Perhaps you might share some insight on what happened?' asked Alice who already realised this sounded like a strange question to be asking the widow of someone who had died a few weeks ago. It was obvious from Kimberly's response that she thought so too.

'Are you Mrs Marple or something. Why do you want to know?' with a certain distain in her tone.

'No dear, I was simply curious as I know that he had a different plan for this holiday.'

Kimberly did a mini recoil action in her seat to convey surprise.

'Really, that is an odd thing to say. What do you know of my husband's plans?'

'Well, I know that he did not expect to end up as fish food that night' blurted Alice.

Kimberly rolled her long neck on her thin formed shoulders. First one way, then the other almost like a Yoga limbering up exercise. Her long hair was tied up with hair pins that exposed and exaggerated the features of her long, thin neck.

Alice felt something click in her mind like a switch of some kind. Definitely not her short scraggy neck though. Or at least she hoped not.

'I'm so sorry Kimberly, I don't know what just came over me. I apologise for being so rude and inquiring on your husband. It's none of my business.'

Kimberly stared at this strange old woman noticing that she was eyeing her up and down. It was a similar look that she got from many of David's lusty friends.

'Really. Its fine, perhaps we should just leave it at that' said Kimberly as she tried to get her skirt confined long legs under her so she could stand up.

'No don't go yet' said Alice leaning forward surprisingly quickly while placing a hand onto Kimberly's thigh.

Kimberly instinctively sat back down. Her hand was now holding Alice's hand in a strange, confusing way. For Kimberly, like a mother. For Alice, like unrequited love.

Alice felt the arousal and strange attraction to this woman she did not know before this night. Her mind was confused. She heard voices somewhere in the distance that she did not recognise. She felt the presence of someone else. A male. A strong man.

'Are you feeling alright' asked Kimberly breaking Alice's thought momentarily.

'Yes, I think so. Perhaps I could just get a glass of water'.

Kimberly looked around the room for a moment.

'Let's get out of this public area. I have some cold water in the fridge in my office and we can have some privacy.'

Each woman helped the other to their feet for different reasons and made their way a short distance to a private office door. Kimberly punched in a code into the keypad and both ladies entered the office to sit at a small meeting table.

'So, tell me Alice. What is it you want to know?'

Alice had a different look about her now. She looked the same person but the glint in her eye, her posture, the smirk across her face said different.

'Your husband. How exactly did he end up overboard Kimberly?'

Now Kimberly was surprised. She narrowed her eyes that brought her fake eyebrows down from her shiny forehead.

'Perhaps he had too much to drink and went out on deck and fell overboard.'

'That is convenient. Perhaps the wrong person went over that night.'

Kimberly was looking intently at the old woman now.

'Really. Are you suggesting that someone else was supposed to drown that night? What would you know anyway, you old crone coming here making accusations?'

'Ssshh.... Do not get upset. What I know stays in this room. I just want to know what happened.'

Kimberly started to compose herself. She shook her hair from

DEREK FINN

side to side, from one shoulder to the other. A hair clip fell out and to the ground causing Kimberly's long hair to drop down on one side.

Alice picked it up and stood to her feet. She walked around the back of Kimberly and placed her hands on her exposed shoulders.

'Here, let me fix it for you.'

Kimberly felt a surprising strength in the hands as they rubbed her shoulders. Slowly and gently, like, like that of a man. A man like Philip Burns.

Alice's mind fired again that caused her to shake her head from side to side. As though to shake a thought loose from the brain. She felt arousal as she touched the skin of Kimberly.

Alice moved her hands to around the front of Kimberly's throat. As she did, she picked up the letter opener from the adjacent desk and slowly placed the tip to the soft part of the throat.

'Your husband was a good man to me. He did not deserve to die.'

Kimberly kept her eyes closed as Alice pressed the tip of the letter opener deeper into her throat.

SUCCESSION PLANNING

Perhaps we are destined to be where we are. If so, then we have no choice in life's outcomes and that decisions are illusions that we have no real control over.

Alice B stared into the remnants of her near empty coffee cup. She knew that her biological clock was counting down, that time had almost run out for her frail body. To be fair, it had served her well for the last eighty years – she did not have too much to complain about. She finished writing up her journal before looking up to see the young Philip Burns enter the coffee shop. As he turned from the serving counter, she made eye contact with him and signalled him to join her table.

'Good morning Philip, surprised you're here so early'

'I was in the area at my therapy sessions that you organised for me' he responded as he sat down on the hard-wooden chair.

'Ah yes, of course. And how are you finding the counselling sessions?' she asked.

'It's ok, I suppose. There seems to be a lot of stating the obvious to be honest.'

Alice smiled and looked at her young protégé. He was a fit young man who had a bad start in life. It crossed her mind momentarily that if she could have his youth and physicality with her intelligence and life experience, that could be a perfect solution for them both.

Later that afternoon, she was at her office when she had a

call to say that her regular physician, Doctor Ryan was missing presumed drowned. Although not surprised, she was nonetheless saddened by the news and wondered if she should contact Doctor Ryan's widow to express her condolences. She decided to make a note to send flowers on behalf of the company instead as a more appropriate gesture. He was a good man after all she thought.

Alice made herself comfortable on the laboratory sized bed and adjusted her hospital smock. She always hated the pre-trial preparations with the research assistants swarming around her, poking, prodding, like she was a piece of meat. Perhaps she was just that she thought to herself. A young nurse stretched across Alice's face to adjust something instead of just walking around the bed.

She had the urge to smack the Nurse across the face for her rudeness. Alice chose to close her eyes instead and let it pass. As she did so, she felt a twinge in her plastic jointed hip that she had had replaced weeks ago. She wondered how much longer this old body of hers could last before completely falling apart.

Poor Doctor Ryan she thought. I will give his lovely wife Kimberly a ring later.

Alice felt the warm infusion of an intravenous cocktail enter her arm. Her eyes flickered momentarily as she felt her body relax and her mind start to swirl. She knew it would not take long now as her mind slipped away into a dream world.

For Alice, it was just a moment. She went from white bed linen to somewhere else in an instant. Her unconscious mind presented her with images, sounds and sensations that the brain could not distinguish as real or dream. She stood before a large carousel that was in full motion.

Although she had never been, it somehow reminded her of the carousel in Central Park New York – so loud and garish.

Lights blinked as the wooden horses circled the millions of mirror tiles at the centre. It was night-time here. And it was cold. Alice looked to each side of her and noticed that there were children watching the carousel making its circular path. Their faces absorbed some of the garish lights reflected outwards from the carousel.

Behind her, she thought she heard someone call her name that caused her to look quickly over her shoulder. It was dark behind and it took a second for her eyes to readjust. Unable to see anyone, she dismissed the call and turned back to watch the happy scene of wooden painted horses galloping a fixed path.

A small person, a child, appeared suddenly beside her. Alice looked down on the child whose arm was outstretched offering something to Alice. She bent forward and took a red string chord from the child. The chord trailed off into the blackness behind her and Alice was uncertain. She hesitated. She looked off into the distance to see as far as she could. The child beside her pointed in the direction of the red string before skipping away.

Alice adjusted herself and followed the red string out across the dark grass. It felt damp underneath or perhaps just cold. Her sensations mixed with her rising fear of what might be at the end of this red string path.

As Alice pulled the string through her fingers, she followed further away from the carousel scene until the sounds and lights had faded away completely. She came to an office door that she instantly recognized. The glazed door glass read PHILIP BURNS Project Manager TDS Limited.

As she walked into the small office in a building premises that she recognized, she was greeted by the young Mr Burns in his dapper blue suit and white shirt. He jumped up from his office chair to greet his visitor. Alice was confused. This was not an experience like any of her past dream visits where she was only an invisible observer through the mind of someone else.

Clearly, Philip could see her, he could hear her, and it was like he expected her to be here.

'Thanks for coming in today' the young Philip gestured her towards a seat.

Alice accepted the offer and sat down fixing her white lab smock trying to stretch it further down to cover more of her aged leather skin legs.

'I am profoundly grateful for this opportunity' Philip continued. 'Your sacrifice for science and this organization will probably go unnoticed by wider society, but you have my thanks.'

Alice had a confused look on her face. She recalled the last time she saw Philip Burns was at the Determination Meeting at TDS' offices in connection with the Susan Birchfield debacle. Where he had gone off plan and beaten the client to death. In fact, I thought he was suffocated at that meeting with a plastic bag over his head.

'What the fuck is going on?' asked Alice.

'I know. I know it's confusing, but a wonderful thing has happened' exclaimed Philip as he pulled his leather office seat closer to his desk. Leaning on his elbows he placed his knotted hands under his chin and smiled across at Alice. Around his pinkie finger, was tied the red string she had followed in all her dreams. She realised that all dreams, all her visions had led to this moment. All had led to Philip Burns.

'There is no easy way to say this, but you are no longer the Alice Braithward that you once were.'

Alice was still confused. This confusion mixed with an unexpected anger that built inside of her. It felt raw. Almost uncontrollable.

'You might experience cognitive dissonance, a slight confusion, for a few minutes as you try to process what has happened' continued Philp in a calm voice that did nothing to calm Alice.

Alice felt a weakness come over her. Suddenly, without warning she experienced a mind shock that traversed down her neck, to her arm, to her wrist. Her arm jerked involuntarily.

Philip pushed his chair back from the desk. It rolled slowly away from the desk.

'Stay calm Alice, it's just a mind shock. It will pass in a moment like it has done many other times.'

Alice looked up and across the table at Philip. He looked the same and yet different. His voice was the same, yet his words did not sound like him.

'But how do you know about the mind shocks?'

'Because I used to have them' he said.

The old woman felt a tightness across her chest. Her mind swirled and fired in confusion. A lightning storm raged across the plains of her mind. Signals pulsed on multiple emotion centres at the same time. Anger, confusion, sadness, happiness, and everything in between. She heard voices in her head speak to her. They shouted abuse and profanity.

'Let me try to explain in terms that you might be able to understand. Your brain, with its intelligence and experience, its wonderful agility and neuroplasticity is now my brain. In my youthful, strong, athletic body. The old body of Alice now has the psychopathic, underdeveloped, damaged brain of Philip Burns'.

The old woman now seethed with uncontrollable anger constrained in the frail body as she looked across the table at the smiling face. She recognised the best of Alice combined with the best of Philip looking back at her.

Another Mind Shock struck the old woman and she winced as the pulse ran through her like electricity.

'You see, you did not suffocate me at our meeting. You are looking through the eyes of an old woman with the damaged brain of a psychopathic young man. The brain swap was partially completed some 22 weeks ago and well before that meeting to test physical and mental compatibility. As I or you, used to say. People see and hear what they want to hear.'

The third and final Mind Shock jolted the frail body of Alice. The doctors attempted resuscitation, but it was fruitless. All EEG monitors showed zero brain activity in the old woman.

Without brain activity, her lungs stopped, and the heart followed suit and ceased to beat. Alice's body finally surrendered to the disease of old age and gave up the good fight. Her brain, her mind, and her essence now resided in another domain mixed with remnants of madness. It was called Philip Burns.

Within months of the passing of Alice Braithward, CEO, Philanthropist and Research Pioneer, she was succeeded in her role by the young and formidable Philp Burns. He transitioned into the role with surprising ease. At least according to outsiders not part of the business.

ABOUT THE AUTHOR

Derek Finn

Derek is a graduate of WIT and University College Cork with a Post Graduate in Applied Psychology. He lives in Ireland and used to be an avid runner. Now he's a jogger and runs only for exercise.

Derek works with different voluntary sectors primarily in psychology and counselling.

BOOKS BY THIS AUTHOR

Natural Frequency

A book of short stories told through the characters of an Irish Witch and her Manic Pigeon. This book is dark humor and sarcasm told through a character that knows what she wants and speaks her mind to get it.

Wildest Moments

This is the second book in the short stories series. This book is written in the time of the pandemic and lock downs and follows the Witch as she experiences lock down isolation with her companions.

Printed in Great Britain
by Amazon